KASH & HEAVEN 2

LOVED BY A STREET SAVAGE

BY

NA'COLE

KASH & HEAVEN 2: LOVED BY A STREET SAVAGE

KASH & HEAVEN 2: LOVED BY A STREET SAVAGE

ONE

The way Esha drove on I290 expressway into downtown Chicago, you would've sworn she was a NASCAR driver. It only took them about twenty minutes to reach Heaven's brand-new abode, and they were both excited to see her new beginnings. This apartment wasn't anything permanent. In all honesty, Sno had Heaven on a three-month lease, but if she wanted to stay longer, he was prepared to provide her with an extended stay.

"Damn, Daddy Sno don't play when it comes to his Sweet Pea." Esha smiled, staring at a beautiful, grey, twenty story building near Roosevelt Road and Michigan Avenue, not too far from the expensive stores and heavy traffic. Both of their mouths were wide open as they pulled up to the front of the building and parked. Turning the blinkers on, they sat there idly, looking out the windows, peeping their surroundings. It was quiet and clean, not the usual scenery in Chicago, especially not the side of town Esha grew up on. So, Esha could appreciate Heaven's new neighborhood, especially since it looked so different from what she remembered growing up. Her freshman year of high school, she took public transportation a few feet away from Heaven's building. Back then, this building was part of a construction site.

"What floor are we going to?" Esha asked, mumbling. Her voice seemed to trail off.

"The eighteenth," Heaven announced as she looked down into her phone at Sno's text message that detailed everything she needed to know about the building.

"I used to stand right there at the bus stop every morning my freshman year of high school. It ain't shit but white people and rich niggas living down here now. I know the rent for your apartment is expensive as fuck."

"The bus stop?" Heaven frowned, bewildered. She'd never had to ride public transportation a day in her life. She could only imagine the struggle Esha went through, having to sit on a crowded bus with all types of smells and undiagnosed diseases floating around.

"Yes, my little rich friend, the bus stop. Rain, sleet, and snow." Esha pinched Heaven's cheek and smiled.

"Esha, shut up." She laughed. "I have you know I've rode the bus a time or two myself."

"Yeah, right! It's okay not to be poor, friend. It's okay not to be privy to struggle. There's nothing cool about it, and you don't have to coddle my feelings. I rode the bus back in the day, but I'm doing all I can to make sure my son doesn't have to," Esha explained.

"You don't have to lie to kick it, Heaven."

"I'm not lying."

"Anyways, all that shit you have in the trunk,

how are we supposed to move it upstairs to your apartment?"

"I only have four suitcases. And we are modern women. We are strong women. We don't need a man for nothing." Heaven pursed her lips. "We got this."

"Says the girl with butlers and shit."

"Butlers? Girl, I don't have any butlers." Heaven laughed.

"Girl, yes the fuck you do, but whatever! Speak for yourself. I do need my man for everything. Hell, you better not need no nigga after how you did Kash." She looked back at Baby Lance briefly before she turned back around to look at Heaven, who was now texting her father.

"Girl, fuck Kash. I just realized I don't have keys to get into my apartment." Heaven grimaced, waiting on Sno to reply.

"Soooo?" Esha looked at Heaven curiously. "What are we supposed to do now? I can't just sit here. I don't have time for CPD today. We need to make a move." As Esha said that, a security officer from the building came outside. They watched as he looked at the truck suspiciously, inspecting it before walking over and knocking on the window.

"I know like hell you are not knocking on my window!" Esha yelled, letting the window down.

"What's up?" she asked, frowning.

"You can't park right here." He knelt, looking into the truck. The security officer was a young guy with long blonde hair that was pulled back into a ponytail. He was a tall, white man with skin the color of a white peach. He wasn't all that cute, but his grey eyes were beautiful. Esha and Heaven frowned as he looked into the truck with authority.

"First of all, I live here," Heaven said.

"And secondly, back the hell up." Esha cocked her head to the side. "Niggas out here with coronavirus, and you got your face all in my shit. Where the fuck is your mask?"

"Look, ma'am, you cannot park here," he said as he stepped back slightly. "Whether you live here or not, you need to move your vehicle before I call the police."

"Now, what the hell are you going to call the police for?"

"Because this is a no parking zone." He pointed at the sign.

"Okay, and I am new to the building and Chicago…"

"Girl, you don't have to explain yourself to him." Esha rolled the window back up. "Call my man and ask him where the parking lot is."

"Who? Lance?"

"No, bitch, your daddy. Mr. Wright." Esha stuck her tongue out.

"Bitch, stop playing with my father." Heaven laughed. "I have the parking info."

"Alright, cool, put it in the GPS," Esha said. Looking out the window, she saw the security officer on his walkie talkie. "Girl, look at his goofy ass. Hurry up." After Heaven put in the address to the parking lot, which was located on Roosevelt and Wabash, directly on the side of the building, Esha turned her blinkers off. Before she pulled from the curb, she honked her horn at the security officer who was standing there with his arms folded across his chest, looking at the truck. She let the window down. "Hey, Mr. Officer, fuck you!" she yelled, holding her middle finger up before driving away.

A couple of minutes later, they were pulling into the parking lot, and Heaven instructed Esha on where to park. Sno paid for her to have two extra parking spots, so she had three in total, but two were already occupied. A white, 2020 Bentley truck was in her spot, while a beautiful, shiny blue, 1986 Oldsmobile Cutlass Supreme was parked in the other.

"Park right there." Heaven pointed to the open space on the side of the Cutlass.

"Are you sure?" Esha pursed her lips. "I don't want my truck getting towed outta here."

"Yes, I'm sure. My daddy said I have three parking spots. I'm guessing the Bentley truck is mine, but that old ass car right there doesn't look familiar. Looks like I'ma have to call Mr. Officer to get it towed."

Esha parked and popped the trunk. "I don't like how you be calling your daddy 'Daddy'." Esha laughed as she stepped from the truck.

"What do you mean? That's my father. What do you call your father?"

"I call him by his name. He ain't nobody special."

"My daddy is my heart. What should I call him?" Heaven frowned as she exited the truck.

"Call him Sno because that's my daddy. Him and your fine ass uncle."

"Girl, shut up." Walking to the trunk, Heaven pulled two suitcases, with wheels at the bottom, out.

"Yo' country ass." Esha laughed. "You know your daddy and uncle are sexy… Anyways, y'all should have a dolly or something to put all your bags on."

Esha walked around to the back passenger door. She opened it and reached inside to retrieve Baby Lance's carrier. Wrapping it around her body and fastening the latches, she unbuckled a sleeping Baby

Lance from his car seat and put him inside.

"I'm not in the mood to do all of that. I only have four suitcases anyways. I got two; you can just grab one since you have my godson in your arms, and I will call my Uncle Blu to come over to get the other one," she said as her phone began to chime. A text message from Sno showed on her phone, letting her know to go to the front desk with her ID, and they would give her her keys.

"Blu is not gonna come all the way over here just to get one suitcase."

"Yes, he is. I'm his favorite niece. Plus, I'm sure my father appointed him to look over me while I'm here. He talked all that shit about me being an adult and looking after myself, but I'm not stupid."

"So, that means I'ma be seeing Mr. Blu very often while you're here. Ahhh, shit, I'ma be over here every day." Esha laughed. "Overstaying my welcome and everything."

It took Heaven all of ten minutes to get her set of keys, and five minutes later, she was unlocking and twisting the doorknob to her new place.

She opened the door and was in tears. The long hallway was filled with black and white pictures of her and Kamelia on the wall. Black and white artwork hung there as well, along with black décor.

"Heaven," Esha said in awe. "This is the first time ever that I've seen someone move into a fully furnished apartment. It is so pretty in here, and we are only at the entrance."

"My Auntie Jayla deserves a trophy for this. Look at my baby." Heaven smiled softly. The floor was covered in grey hardwood with specks of white, black, and silver throughout. She knew Jayla had nothing to do with the color of the floors; however, she did a good job matching her decorations.

Walking from the hallway, they entered the entryway of the kitchen and living room. A tall island with two stools separated the stainless-steel appliances in the kitchen from the black décor in the living room. A leather sectional sat along the window with black, red, and white furry pillows on top. In the center of the room was a black fur rug and a black fur throw blanket was thrown on the arm of the couch. Black, silver, and red curtains hung in the tall picture windows that showed parts of Michigan Avenue. In Atlanta, Heaven lived in a house, a beautiful home that she decorated herself. Living in an apartment was sort of a downgrade; however, Jayla had her in tears. The way she hooked her apartment up had her emotional.

"Who is this Jayla person, and how can I hire her?" Esha asked. She had lived in Chicago almost her entire life, but she never had the opportunity to live in this type of luxury. The rent for this apartment had to run Heaven at least four thousand dollars a month. Even the home Esha lived in in Park Ridge, Illinois did not compare to Heaven's living arrangements. Her apartment was the shit on its own, but Jayla's interior decorating skills brought it out more. Plus, Heaven was living amongst music artists, athletes, and even reality show personalities. Esha prayed that she bumped into somebody famous while she was walking out.

"Jayla is Reign's best friend. I don't think you know her."

"Oh, yeah. I remember seeing her around the house, but I don't know her. I just know Marie."

"Jayla is married to my Uncle Blu."

"Girl," Esha said, rolling her eyes. She didn't really want to be with Sno or Blu for real, but she did fantasize about them both. They were both handsome men, but she knew things couldn't go past her liking them. "All the fine niggas are taken. I don't like that."

"Esha, you are so ungrateful. You have a fine nigga already. So, leave my daddy and uncle alone,"

Esha stomped her feet and pouted, causing Baby Lance to stir from his sleep. He looked up at Esha and smiled "But why?"

"Look at you, done woke the baby up. Let's go and check out the bedrooms." Heaven laughed, grabbing ahold of Esha's hand. When Heaven and Esha entered the hallway, they heard the toilet flush. Startled, they gripped each other's hand tightly.

"Who the fuck is that?" Esha asked, whispering.

"I don't know. It might be an automatic toilet." Heaven grimaced.

"But why is the door closed?"

"Let's go find out." Heaven began to tiptoe towards the door. "Come on, Esha."

"Hell no. You acting real white right now." Esha ran behind a wall to one of the bedrooms. "Heaven, get yo' ass over here."

"Shhhh." Heaven put her index finger to her lip and lifted her other hand to open the door. Before she could twist the knob, the door swung open and out walked Jayla, fixing her dress while Blu kissed her neck.

"Aaahhhh!" Heaven screamed and jumped back. Next to the bedroom Esha was hiding in was the second bedroom, which was where Heaven ran to.

"Aaahhh," Jayla screamed aloud too, as well as Esha. Baby Lance began crying out loud, and Blu looked up from Jayla's neck, seemingly unbothered.

"Heaven!" she yelled, placing her hand to the bottom of her belly as her baby began to move around. "You

about to send me into labor."

"Jayla? Uncle Blu? What are y'all doing here? In the bathroom." She stepped out from the bedroom.

"Don't tell me y'all just got done having sex in there." She frowned. They both looked guilty as sin, and Heaven shook her head, thinking she didn't even get the chance to bless her own apartment first.

"Gaddamn, Heaven. You can't be sneaking up on us like that," Blu said, getting off the subject. He walked over to Heaven and hugged her. "What's been going on, niece?"

"Nothing. Y'all stink," Heaven said, laughing as she and Blu continued to embrace.

"Girl, I bet you lying." Jayla laughed and hugged Heaven as well.

"I thought I heard a baby crying." Blu looked over Heaven's head in the direction of the master bedroom as Esha peeped out.

"Is it safe to come out?" she asked, stepping out. Seeing Blu's face let her know things were safe. She walked over to the trio with Baby Lance now on her hip.

As Heaven and Jayla unwrapped from their embrace, Esha smiled lustfully at Blu.

"Who is your friend, Heaven?"

"Oh." Heaven pursed her lips and put her arm over Esha's shoulder. "This is my friend, Esha. Y'all met years ago, Uncle."

"Hey, Blu." Esha smiled shyly.

"What's up?"

"Nah uhn!" Jayla frowned, grabbing ahold of Blu's arm. She didn't like the way Esha was looking at her husband.

"Jayla, this is Reign's old neighbor, my best friend, Esha."

"Mmm, hey there."

"Wow," Esha said under her breath. Now, Esha was a bitch, but Jayla was something else. She was an even bigger bitch. Esha surmised it was Jayla's pregnancy hormones causing her to act this way. "Hi, Jayla. Nice to meet you."

"Blu, I'll be in the front. See you later, Heaven

girl."

"Okay, big mama." Heaven hugged Jayla and rubbed her stomach before she walked off.

"We're about to go ahead and get outta here. Sno asked us to come over and check on you," Blu announced. "Did you need anything before we leave? Your truck is parked in the lot next to my old school. Did you see it?"

"Oh, that was your blue car. I should've known. I just need you to get my bag from Esha's truck."

"Aight, I got you... Give me another hug, niece," he said before hugging Heaven again. "It was nice seeing you again, Esha."

After hearing the front door close, Heaven and Esha walked back into the living room. Esha put Lance down on the floor as she walked over to the windows with Heaven on her heels. They looked outside at the stores and businesses in the neighborhood. Clothing stores, restaurants, and hotels surrounded the area. A little further down Roosevelt Road, the 12th Street beach, near the boats and yachts, caught Heaven's attention. The water was so blue and clear. This was a great area to live.

"I like Jayla. She is mean as hell." Esha turned her head to look at Heaven. She smiled.

"Yes, she's even meaner when it comes to Blu. My te-te was about to beat your ass over her husband. My auntie said, 'Play with your mammy because playing with her ain't safe'."

"Nah, I would rather play with her man."

"You are something else, bestie. I don't know what you women see in him or my father."

"I told you already. Those two niggas are sexy as fuck. Think about it this way. The same way you look at Kash, all googly eyed and shit, is the same way we look at your father and uncle."

They both laughed for different reason. Esha was just silly, and she found the way she made Heaven feel awkward hilarious, while Heaven understood because she definitely looked at Kash admirably. Not only was he sexy and a go getter, but he had given her a huge piece of him when they made Kamelia.

***

Heaven's day had been long and full of emotions. She couldn't believe how she was so mentally affected by seeing Kash. Why couldn't she just be bold enough to claim what she felt was hers? The sound of his voice, his entire face, even the feel of his hand against her face when he gripped her chin made her quiver. It was something about the way he carried himself that made Heaven want him, but she refused to be foolish. Closing her eyes and laying her head back against the couch, she saw Kash's face with his lips up against her forehead as he held her in his arms. No one ever had this type of effect on her. She wished she would've been able to control her feelings in front of him. In front of his little girlfriend. In her eyes, showing those types of emotions were for the weak. Now, Kash, Lance, Asia, and the entire block knew exactly how she felt about him. They knew she loved him and was torn over seeing him with another woman.

"What you thinking about?" Esha asked as she turned to Heaven and sat Indian style on the couch. She put her elbows into her thighs and her fists underneath her chin. She was curious to know because, for the past few seconds, she had been calling Heaven's name, and Heaven didn't respond.

"Nothing."

"You are lying, Heaven. You can tell me. I won't say anything out loud that the world doesn't already know."

Heaven sucked her teeth. "Kash and everything that happened today. I looked like a fool crying over him."

"First of all, you didn't look like a fool. If anything, he looked crazy, punching my window and shit. Remind me to kick his ass later."

"Yeah, that was crazy."

"That damn girl he had with him looked like a damn fool. Sitting there, letting her nigga go stupid over a girl... No, not a girl because bitch, you are all woman. So, let me rephrase that. She stood there and watched her nigga go crazy over a woman he ain't seen in over five years."

Heaven smiled at Esha; she was so happy to know Esha wasn't judging her. After the day she had today, she needed to hear this.

"I appreciate that, Esha. I guess I wasn't ready to see him. I don't know."

"You was ready to see him. You just wasn't ready to see that he had moved on with someone else," Esha said honestly. She could understand how Heaven felt. She hadn't been through it personally; still, she understood.

"Does she have children?" Heaven asked, sighing. She didn't want to know, but she needed to know.

"I don't know. I don't know her. I've heard of her. Lance told me the bitch is loco. But today was the first time I've seen her."

"Do you know her name?"

"Her name is Asia. Why?"

"No reason."

"No reason my ass. Because what we are not about to do is look this bitch up on social media. She's not worth it. The bitch doesn't have enough money to live in your mind. Especially if Kash's relationship with her will determine what type of relationship you allow him to have with Kamelia."

Heaven sighed and looked down at her cell, her finger hovering over the 'A' in contempt. She wanted to look Asia's page up so bad. She needed to know specific things about Asia and Kash's relationship. She needed to know if he was playing daddy and hubby, but she knew Esha wouldn't let her. In her heart, she knew Esha was right.

"Heaven Wright, close that Facebook app," Esha said. "Because I love you, I will not let you do this to yourself. Maybe she does have kids. And maybe Kash is a part of their lives, but that's what comes along with the territory. She and her kids, if she has any, are a package deal."

Hearing those words caused Heaven to become

emotional. They flooded her, causing her chest to tighten and her eyes to become misty.

"Awwww, don't cry, friend," Esha said, wiping at Heaven's face as a tear escaped one eye. "You're just overly sensitive right now, but you will be okay. Trust me."

"I'm not sensitive. I'm hurt."

"You say tomato; I say tomato. Same shit!" Esha said, causing Heaven to laugh through her tears. "See, look at that beautiful smile."

"Esha, you are so silly."

"I know!" Esha pinched Heaven's cheek and stood from the couch. She stretched her body, bending over to touch her toes before walking over to the window and looking out.

"Heaven, you are one lucky girl. I just pray you see that one day soon."

"Where did that come from?" Heaven frowned as she wiped her face and turned the TV down. Sitting up, she turned to look at Esha. She knew her life was great, lavish, and luxurious, but she wouldn't call her situation with Kash lucky. None of the material things she had could cure the pain she felt in her heart.

"I'm just saying. You have a beautiful life, Heaven. You have everything you want and more. If you wanted to, you could go to build a nigga and create the perfect gentleman."

"If only it was that simple."

"Yes, bitch. I'm just talking shit, but seriously, give Kamelia a family. You grew up with your father in your life; she deserves the same. Kash wants to be there. That shit ain't common nowadays. I know how you feel about him but put that to the side and give your baby what is rightfully hers. Hell, if that Asia bitch does have kids, it's time for Kamelia to take her father. He belongs to her. And if you want him, take his ass."

"I love you, Esha." Heaven stood and walked over to the window. Through tears and all, she hugged Esha.

"I love you too, Heaven."

TWO

Kash's mind was stuck on Heaven as he sat next to Asia on the couch in her living room, staring at the TV. To the left of him sat Asia's son, Taiwan, while Malaysia and India sat on the floor watching the Disney movie Asia had turned on thirty minutes earlier. With her head on his chest, and his hand gripping her hip, they looked like the perfect family.

Being around Asia and her kids like this always made him think about Heaven and Kamelia. And after seeing Heaven today, that made him think even more. Kash knew he had to find out where she lived, so he could pay her a visit. They needed to talk alone. Away from prying eyes and nosey ears.

Raising his arm up, he looked at his watch. It was a little after 10 p.m., and he just realized he hadn't gone to check on the girl Dre asked him to. "Shit," he said under his breath. After everything that happened earlier, he wanted to put Asia's mind at ease. So, she took him to pick up his car, and he trailed her home where they spent the rest of the day hanging out with her kids.

"What's wrong?" Asia asked, noticing his disposition.

Ding! Kash's phone chimed.

Dre: What's up, Kash? Did you handle that business?

"Damn," he whispered.

Kash: I just looked at the time. I'm on my way now.

Dre: G, her plane landed hours ago.

Kash: I know. That's my bad. I'm on it though.

"Kash!" Asia yelled.

"What?"

"What's wrong?"

"I have to go."

"Right now? We're in the middle of watching a movie with the kids."

"I know, but I have some business to handle."

Asia sat up from his chest and looked at him. What type of business did he have to handle right now? It was very late in the evening, and she was hoping they could put the kids to bed and lay up.

"Kash, don't give me that handle some business bullshit." Things sounded very suspicious, especially since his little baby mama was in town. "We are your business right now. Me, Malaysia, India, and Taiwan."

"Asia, don't do that in front of the kids, man."

"Fuck these kids!" she yelled, and all three turned to look at her. "I fucked up getting pregnant in the first place."

"Asia, shut the fuck up. Don't say that dumb ass shit in front of them," he said, attempting to stand from the couch, but Asia pulled at his arm.

"You don't give a fuck about my kids. So, stop acting like you do. All you care about is yourself. You're just trying to go meet up with your baby mama."

Kash yanked his arm away and stood up. "Come here, man." He pulled her up by her arm. "Come talk to me in the room." He didn't feel the need to explain anything to her, and he wasn't. He wanted to get down to the root of her problems.

"No, Kash, fuck you," she cried. "I don't have shit to say to you."

"I don't like how you're doing this in front of your kids."

"Because they are my fucking kids." She spoke. Kash grabbed her and pulled her to him. He shook his head, not understanding her outburst. He hadn't given her a reason to think he was on his way to see Heaven. He honestly didn't know where Heaven was staying.

Picking Asia up, he walked her to the bedroom and placed her on her feet. Cupping her face in his hand, he looked into her face. He had to wonder how he attracted such a toxic woman who clearly hated her own kids. Looking at her, all he could imagine was his mother and how she treated him as a kid.

"Kash, you don't love me." She pushed at his chest, and he allowed her.

"Asia, you gotta chill, man." He took a deep breath before grabbing her hands. "I care for you. But you don't love yourself. I've been here with you. I try to build something with you, but it's never enough. Still, I give you everything you want. I give your kids me and my time - something I don't even give my own daughter." He looked her in her eyes.

"It's not my fault you're not around your daughter. So, you can stop throwing her in my face, Kash. I can't deal with that shit right now."

"If you can't handle the fact that I have a daughter then whatever we are working towards will never work," he said, and Asia sniffled. "Kamelia and Heaven are both a part of me. I accept your kids so accept mine. I'm not throwing her in your face, but I'm not hiding her either. Heaven is a part of my daughter. She is the woman I created life with, so you have to accept her too. She's going to be in my life regardless."

"Heaven?" Asia scoffed. "Why does she have to be a part of your life too? She's only your child's mother."

"Asia, I don't have to explain that to you. Let's focus on you and the crazy shit you just said in the living room." Asia sucked her teeth and rolled her eyes. "You sat there, in front of your kids, and said fuck them because you thought I was on my way to see another woman when I am literally on my way out to handle some business that I forgot to handle earlier. I'm sitting here, tryna cater to you and your feelings. What about me and mine? I'm missing out on money and shit fucking wit' you."

"I'm sorry," she said sarcastically. Everything Kash said to her went in one ear and out the other. She didn't give a damn about what Kash felt when it came to her own feelings.

"Oh, you wanna be sarcastic? You're sorry? I'm getting tired of your shit, Asia. You talk to the kids crazy as hell. Do you not understand what that type of shit does to a kid?"

"I didn't mean it. I'm just going through so much

right now." She took a step back and sat down on the bed. With her face in her hands, she cried. "I feel depressed… I just don't know what to do. I hate that my kids have to see me like this and even have to deal with my mood swings. Kash, I don't want you to leave me."

"Asia, I didn't say I was going anywhere. I'm here for you. But you need to get yourself together. The way you act scares the fuck outta me. You're not in a good mental space for a relationship, but I'm trying with you." He knelt to her level and hugged her. He honestly felt sorry for her.

Asia kissed Kash's neck and said, "I am in a good head space, Kash. We belong together. Just let me prove it to you."

Kash closed his eyes and sighed before looking into her eyes again. "You can't make me happy if you're not happy. And you definitely can't make me happy if you continue to mistreat Malaysia, India, and Taiwan. No nigga's happiness should come before yours or your kids'."

"You are who makes me happy."

"Don't give me that much credit, Asia. You have to know how to be just as happy without me."

"I don't think I will be able to go on with life without you."

"With or without me, you got this life shit on lock." He cupped her face. Asia was mentally unstable, and Kash knew it. He tried to say all the right words because this conversation was taking a left turn. He kissed her forehead. "I have to go, but I will be right back."

THREE

Heaven's house shoes made a light shuffling noise as she moved around her apartment. After Esha left her alone to her thoughts, she decided she would take a shower before calling it a night. It was now eleven o'clock in the evening, still a little early to be sleeping, but today was a long day. She went into the bathroom, and turned the shower on. Letting the water run as she stepped out into the hallway, closed the bathroom door and ran her fingers through her hair. Yawning, she walked into the kitchen and sighed as she walked over to the refrigerator.

Swinging the door open, she rummaged through the fully stocked fridge. Nothing but healthy food sat inside, but tonight, she didn't want any food. It was more of a cocktail night, and she knew there had to be some wine, champagne, vodka, or something in there. Looking in the back, she found a half full fifth of Remy, and she knew Blu had to have left it by mistake. She blew out a breath and picked it up. Mistake or not, Blu was not getting this bottle back. It was time to unwind.

"Thank you, Uncle Blu." She smiled. She needed this drink. Retrieving a glass from the cabinet, Heaven rinsed it out and poured herself a shot. She felt a little bit like an alcoholic, drinking alone. Still, this was going to help her sleep, especially since she was a little afraid to stay home in Chicago alone.

She threw the shot back, and immediately after, she poured another one. Next, she called Derrick, and they shared stories of their long, adventurous day. Heaven made sure to keep her run in with Kash to herself.

"I walked in on Blu and Jayla doing some nasty shit in my bathroom. I could've thrown up. They are too old to still be fucking," she said, laughing.

"Them old heads be the biggest freaks," he said, He knew this for a fact because, after he woke up from his nap to Anika laying on his chest, he woke her up. She didn't apologize for the position she put him in. Instead, she licked his body and his dick until she made him cum.

Rubbing his chin, he shook his head at the memory, not even paying attention to Heaven's rant. "Your mama came over here looking for you earlier after you left."

"What did she want?"

"Your guess is as good as mine. She was drunk as

hell though," he said, and Heaven gasped, shaking her head. She'd never seen or heard of her mother being drunk before.

"Drunk? That damn guilt must be eating that bitch up."

"What guilt?" He had a feeling Heaven knew about Anika's secret, but he was going to act like he didn't know anything.

"Delilah asked me not to say anything. But this shit has been heavy on my heart. My dad is not her father."

"Word!" He played dumb.

"I'm so hurt, Derrick. My father and my sister are my heart. I can only imagine how Delilah feels right now. And my daddy is going to kill Anika. I'ma have one dead parent and one incarcerated parent."

"I can only imagine,"

Sighing, Heaven said, "Well, I will call you tomorrow. I'm about to call my dad and take a shower."

"Alright, I love…" Before he could get the entire statement out, Heaven hurriedly hung up. She was not about to lie and tell Derrick she loved him.

She poured another shot and threw it back just as quickly as the brown liquor touched the inside of the glass. Afterwards, she walked over to the window with her glass and Blu's Remy in her hands. Looking out, she was in awe of how the city lights made downtown Chicago glow. It was so beautiful outside. It was nothing like what they portrayed on the news. Sitting the Remy and glass down on the windowsill, she stripped out of her sweats. After another shot was in her glass, she held it to her lips as she searched for Asia on social media.

Immediately, a sponsored photo of Asia and Kash displayed. Heaven instinctively curled her fist tightly around her phone, ready to break. The amount of physical strength seeing this picture caused her to have was crazy. She wished this phone was Kash's face, or even Asia's. She was ready to see blood.

"Calm down, Heaven." Her voice shook and so did her hand.

Heaven clicked on Asia's name and saw she had posted another picture twelve minutes ago. This one was of her, Kash, and three small kids laid up in bed.

"Oh my God!" she yelled as tears instantly began to flow. She knew Kash was playing house with Asia. What did Asia and her kids have that she and Kamelia didn't?

Now, she wished she would've listened to Esha. She was all the way in Chicago. She was alone, with hurt feelings and no one to turn to or talk to. She couldn't call and tell Esha because Esha had warned her; and she couldn't tell Sno because he was against her going to Chicago to chase after Kash. Plus, he wasn't there, in Chicago. She needed his chest to cry on the same way she used to as a kid.

Heaven closed the app and fixed herself up before calling Sno's phone. She had to talk to Kamelia. She and Sno were the only two people who made her feel better. She knew he would hear the tears in her voice, and she didn't want to alarm him or get him upset for nothing. Sucking up her tears, she dialed Sno's number. The phone rang once, and he picked up.

"What's going on, Sweet Pea?"

"Hey, Daddy," she said in a low, sorrowful tone.

"What's wrong?"

"Nothing. I had a couple shots with Esha. I'm just a little tipsy."

"You sound more than tipsy. What's up? Did somebody do something to you?"

"No, Daddy." She laughed. "You are so overprotective."

"You damn right I am," he said. "You're my baby girl."

"Any who, where is my baby?"

"Oh, Kamelia is knocked out sleep. She just went to

bed about five minutes ago. I'll let her call you in the morning."

"Yes, please make sure she does."

"After that, you can tell me what's wrong. What has my Sweet Pea in her feelings," Sno said as they both laughed.

Knock! Knock! Knock!

"Daddy," Heaven whispered.

"What?"

"Someone is knocking at my door. Should I answer it?" She was afraid.

"Yeah, answer it."

"Daddy, I'm scared. Who could be knocking so late?"

"It could be someone from the front desk. Go look through the peep hole first."

Heaven tiptoed to the door and looked out.

"I'ma kill Esha," she murmured, sucking her teeth.

"Who's at the door?" Sno asked.

"It's the front desk. I'ma call you tomorrow, Daddy."

"Alright, Sweet Pea. I love you."

"I love you too."

Click.

Heaven looked through the peep hole again and sighed. Seeing Kash standing there, she debated on if she should answer or not. She stood there in nothing but her panties and bra, watching him knock. She refused to let him into her apartment. Who did he think he was, showing up at her home unannounced? And who did Esha think she was, telling Kash where she lived? She watched as Kash looked down into his phone before putting it to his ear.

"Dre, shorty ain't answering the door."

Dre? My daddy sent Kash here? she thought, frowning.

"I don't want to just walk in her crib. Her baby daddy might be here. I'm not tryna walk in on no crazy shit."

"My baby daddy? Kash, what type of games are you tryna play?" she whispered, still looking out the peep hole.

"What's her name? Maybe she'll feel comfortable opening the door if I know her name."

"What is going on?"

"Heaven?" The look on his face as he said her name made her stomach do cartwheels. Heaven watched as Kash took in a breath and brushed his waves down with his hand. This shit had to be a coincidence.

"Aight, G. I'ma call you back."

Kash raised his fist to knock again, but before he could, Heaven opened the door.

45

FOUR

"Kashmir, why are you knocking on my door?" she asked as he looked her body up and down. She'd forgotten she only had her underwear on.

"I came to check on you. I didn't know you were the person I was coming here to see. I would've agreed either way, but I would've made sure you were cool with it first."

Heaven sucked her teeth and put her hand on her hip. Holding the door open with her other hip, she asked, "Who hired you? My father? Does he know who you are? Are y'all setting me up?"

"No, I don't know your father. Dre hired me. Besides, you ain't nobody to be tryna set up."

"Dre hired you? Did my daddy approve this?"

"Does it matter, Heaven? What's with all the damn questions, Jo?"

"You have a woman. Why would you be so

interested in checking on the next bitch?"

Kash responded to Heaven's question with his own question. "Can I come in?"

"Hell no, you may not come in." She frowned. "Go home to little Miss Asia… That's her name, right?"

"Yeah, that's her name."

"Okay, go home to her and her package deal."

"What the fuck are you talking about? Package deal?"

"Her and her fucking kids." Heaven frowned.
"How dare you play father of the year with the next hoe and her little bastards when you're not even a father to your own child, Kashmir?"

Kash hung his head and smirked nervously. "I'm not playing father to nobody."

"Oh, no?"

"No," he said adamantly.

"So, what would you say if I told you I have proof that you're standing in my face lying?"

"I would say fuck your proof because the shit ain't true."

"Okay!" Heaven nodded her head up and down as she unlocked her cell and went to Asia's Instagram page. Kash stood there with his arms folded across his chest.

"What are you searching for?" He just knew Heaven was on some bullshit.

"Calm down, Mr. Family Man. I'm about to show you." After she located the picture, she shoved her cell into his face. And just like before, her eyes began to well with tears.

Kash took the phone from her hand and stared at it. He was speechless. He knew seeing this picture had to hurt Heaven's feelings.

"I had nothing to do with this picture. This had to be this morning when I was sleep."

"Look at you and your family," Heaven said through her tears. "If you were a father to your real daughter, she would be in this picture too with her step siblings and stepmother."

"Man, you tryna be funny?"

"No. I'm being for real," she said, looking up at him. "Why are you so comfortable with another man's kids but haven't asked about your own daughter in the past five years?" Tears were now dripping from her chin.

"Come here, man." He grabbed her around her waist, and she pushed at his chest, trying to fight him off.

"No, Kash. You got to be a bold ass nigga to be posted up on social media with her daughters like this."

"Heaven, trust me when I tell you I knew nothing about this picture. I spend time with Asia and her kids, but that's it. I'm not tryna play father or nothing ike that. I've been tryna get you to talk to me for years now. I have a thousand pictures of you and Kamelia in my phone." He pulled his phone out and went to the pictures he had of Heaven and Kamelia saved to his favorites. Giving her his phone, he allowed her to scroll.

"You have no idea how fucked up I feel about missing five years of my daughter's life. Any woman I fucked with after you, I make sure I strap up," he said, lifting her face from the phone and looking at her as he spoke honestly. "I would never want to give another child what I didn't give my first."

"These pictures and what you're saying doesn't mean shit to me, Kash," she lied, shoving his phone back into his hand. Honestly, everything he was saying dried her tears. She knew he meant every word he was saying.

"It does matter, and I know you believe me. I want to meet my daughter, and if possible, I want you and I to start all over. I know I left a bad taste in your mouth in the past, but I… I can show you the type of man I really am." Heaven didn't respond. She just watched his lips as he stumbled over his words. "Do you hear me?"

"Yes, I hear you. But fuck you. You've hurt me over and over. You didn't want shit to do with me or our daughter, Kash."

"I can't take back what I've done in the past. I can only show you different starting now." He walked closer to her. "I been standing out here, pouring my heart out to you, and all you can say is fuck me. Aight, fuck me. I accept that. But this shit ain't about me. It's about forgiveness, and I forgave you for not letting me see my daughter."

"You didn't deserve to see her. You left her."

"But I asked about her. I tried to get Esha to give me your phone number."

"I know, and I told her not to. I didn't want to talk to your ass." She wiped the last remanence of her tears away.

"So, why are you here now?"

"To give you a chance to meet your daughter. She needs you."

"Exactly. Your mean ass did all that staying away for shit."

Heaven smacked her lips and pushed his shoulder. "I'm not mean."

"You mean as hell, shorty. It's good to see those crocodile tears dried up though." He put his hand to the side of her face.

"My tears are very fucking real. Ain't shit crocodile over here. And I appreciate you pouring your heart out to me. I told myself I was coming to Chicago to resolve our past. I want you to be a part of Kamelia's life. Hell, I want you to be a part of my life, but I can't see us going any further than my front door knowing that you are in a relationship with a girl who has children."

"I'm not in anything committed. Asia can be gone just like that." Kash snapped his fingers as he spoke. He walked all the way up on Heaven and kissed her forehead. She pushed him back.

"Kash, don't touch my face with your pussy eating lips."

"You would know." He laughed, remembering the day he ate her out in the driver's seat of his old ass Ford Explorer.

"Why are you looking at me like that? You don't have permission to look at my body." Placing her arms across her chest, she tried to cover up.

Kash was so into telling Heaven how he felt that he tried his best to keep his eyes on her face and not her body. But the thought of the things they did in the past made his eyes wander and travel down her silhouette.

Kash smirked. "That's cool. You ain't got no ass or hips no way."

"Boy, whatever." She turned around, showing off her plump ass that had swallowed the neon green boy shorts she had on while her childbearing hips protruded slightly. Heaven was thick in all the right places. So, Kash had her fucked up.

"Mmm." He put his index finger and thumb to his chin, admiring her curves. "I see you, shorty." Kash snickered at his cleverness and ability to trick Heaven into willingly showing him her body.

Heaven turned back around quickly, realizing the fast one he'd pulled on her and hit his chest with the palm of her hand. She was still pissed at him. She was still deeply in her feelings. It hadn't even been twenty minutes since she cried her eyes out while downing a glass of Remy because of an obvious bait picture she'd seen of him and his package deal family. But Kash had such a mellow soul. He made her laugh. He made her feel at ease. He just had this crazy hold on her heart. He was talking about them relearning one another, making it a point to tell her Asia wasn't anything serious, so she was curious to see where things would go. Plus, she was very attracted to him. He was an attractive person, inside and out.

"You're gonna make me stand out here all night?"

"First of all, it is almost twelve in the morning. Thank you for checking on me, but I'm sure when Dre hired you, he said nothing about dropping off dick in the middle of the night."

Kash laughed out loud which was something he rarely did. Heaven was something else. Twenty-one year old Heaven was definitely different from sixteen year old Heaven. She was no longer a timid girl. She was now a grown ass woman who spoke her mind.

"Girl, ain't nobody tryna fuck you. Get yo' goofy ass outta here."

"Yeah, right! You took all this time to come through. A few more hours, when it was light outside, wouldn't have hurt you."

Kash sucked his teeth and smirked.

"My man is in the bathroom anyways," she said, looking behind her as if she could see the bathroom from there. "So, you can't come in." She tried to close the door, and he pushed it back open.

"Man, let me in this mafucka." He walked up on her and put his hand on her waist. Without protest from Heaven, Kash forced his way inside, walking her backwards as he looked her directly in her eyes. "You bet not have no nigga in here." He put his lips to hers and kissed her softly. Heaven could've melted from his assertiveness. Him acting as if she belonged to him and looking her in her eyes while he threw out demands was sexy, especially the way his words fell from his lips, in his Chicago accent. That shit made her heart gallop in her chest. And the way he softly kissed her lips, she couldn't deny the fact that his actions alone made her body react. She felt weak.

She was in shock as he released her waist and walked around her. She watched him in pure admiration, through slitted eyes, while her bottom lip was trapped in between her teeth. He pulled his gun off his hip and began walking through her apartment as if he owned it. His size thirteen black and red Air Jordan 13s stomped against the floor swiftly as he rushed to the back of the apartment.

"What are you doing?" she asked, closing the door and locking it. Kash was like a canine, letting his gun lead the way around her apartment, sniffing out any unwanted guest.

"What the fuck it look like I'm doing?"

"Uhm, it looks like you're invading my privacy," she said, following behind him. The bathroom door was closed, and the shower was running .

Assumingely, Kash thought she had a man in there for real.

"You ain't got no fucking privacy, my nigga." Stopping in his tracks, he cocked the hammer of his gun and aimed at the bathroom's door.

"What are you doing, Kash?" she yelled.

Pow! He shot a hole through it.

"Kash!" Heaven screamed, putting her hands to her ears. "I was joking," she said. Still, Kash walked to the door and kicked it open. Instantly, fog from the hot shower began to pour into the hallway. His vision was a little impaired as he ran inside with his gun still pointed, ready to shoot the first thing moving.

"No one is in there, Kashmir," Heaven yelled, and after he checked it out for himself, making sure no other nigga was in there, he put his gun back in his waistband.

"G, I got ADHD. You can't be playing with me like that." He turned around to look at her.

"Yo' crazy ass," she said. Now, she was a little shaken up. The way he reacted to her saying her man was in the bathroom turned her on, but now, she was afraid of how he would act once she told him she was an engaged woman.

"Come here." Kash grabbed Heaven again. This time, he gripped both of her ass cheeks, walking her backwards towards the shower.

"Uhh uhn!" She put her right hand to his chest and held her left hand out as if she was a little kid begging

Daddy for some money. He needed to pay for the door he shot a hole through and kicked off the hinges.

"What?"

"Money, nigga. I have to get this door fixed. My daddy cannot find out what happened here."

"Yo' spoiled ass still scared of your pops? He won't find out. I got you. Do you have Zelle?" Kash asked cleverly.

"Yes." She responded to his question about having a Zelle.

"Aight, what's your phone number? I'ma send it to you."

He pulled his phone out and pretended to go to his banking app. Truthfully, he didn't even have a bank account. He was old fashioned. He preferred to keep his money tucked away in boxes. Instead, he clicked his phone app. As Heaven read off her phone number, he typed it in. Afterwards, he repeated it back, acting like he needed to make sure he was sending the money to the correct account. He pressed talk once he confirmed her phone number and put his phone to his ear, staring at her the entire time.

"708… Who is this?" she asked.

"That bet not be no nigga," he said. One hand was gripping his phone to his ear, and his arm was underneath the other.

"It's not, crazy ass," she replied.

"Well, answer that shit."

Heaven did as she was told. "Hello." She answered and squinted her eyes while pulling the phone from her ear after hearing her voice echo and an ear piercing screech.

"Kashmir, I gave you my phone number to Zelle me, not call me."

He shrugged. "Stop calling me that shit. Call me Killa K." He licked his lips and smiled. Hanging up his phone, he placed it in his pocket.

"Killa K my ass. I am not calling you that shit. I'm not one of your little friends or flunkies."

"I don't have any flunkies, shorty. But I'm tryna make you my best friend." Positioning himself directly in front of her, he put his lips to hers. With his eyes closed, he parted her lips with his tongue and pinned her up against the shower's glass door. He took her top lip into his mouth as she took his bottom lip into hers. Before he could slip his tongue into her mouth again, Heaven bit him and pushed him.

"Whatever, Kash. Just send me my money."

"Damn, G, I'ma send you that lil' paper later. I got you," he said as he put his thumb to his bottom lip and wiped at it. "Feisty ass." He bent down to her level and kissed her neck.

"Kash, stop," she whispered. "My daddy is going to kill me if he finds out about you destroying shit in this apartment."

"I told you I got you. Trust me. I'm good for it." He grabbed her again, pulling her to him.

"What if somebody heard the gunshots? Kash, stop."

"Man, these people don't give a fuck. This is Chicago. Niggas hear gunshots all day every day."

Heaven looked up at him in shock. This was a nice neighborhood that housed individuals with nothing less than six figures in their banking accounts. They couldn't be used to feeling like they were living in a war zone. "Yeah, baby, we really living like that out here. That's why I keep it on me." He looked down at her, his eyes gazing into hers.

"Boy," she sighed. "You keep what on you?" she asked with her lips pursed.

"That's not important. Just know you're safe with me." His nose touched hers, and she took a deep breath.

She believed him. Physically, she was safe with him, but her heart was a different story. As they both looked into each other's eyes, she felt a flutter in her stomach. It was as if they were picking back up where they left off years ago.

She had to get away from him. She wanted him, but it was clear he wasn't an available man, no matter how he tried to feed her that Asia and I aren't anything serious line. She bet he told all the girls that when they inquired about his relationship status.

Nevertheless, Heaven knew what she wanted, and it was Kashmir Harris. She wanted him to love her and take her away from her miserable relationship with Derrick. She wanted everything Kash had to offer - his heart, his life, and his time. She wanted to be in his skin. She wanted to wake up every morning wrapped up in his arms. She wanted to smell his cologne every day before he left home and when he returned. They were all her wants, her needs, but she knew he didn't want the same. She knew exactly what he wanted. It was obvious. He wanted to fuck her. It had been a very long time since their bodies met intimately. In all honesty, she wanted to fuck him too, but she wasn't going to settle with being the other woman. How she saw it, after birthing his big head ass child, she should be his wife, his only woman. This shit here was trifling. He was not about to come to her house at twelve in the morning, have sex with her, and then go home to his little family. That shit wasn't happening.

"Stop, move." She turned her face to the side, and he moved in closer.

"For real for real, you don't really want me to stop." He whispered in her ear while taking her diamond studded earring and earlobe into his mouth.

Oh my God! Don't fuck him, Heaven... Don't give him this good ass head and pussy, Heaven. He doesn't deserve it... Create a distraction, bitch! She screamed at herself in her head.

"I thought you wasn't here to fuck me, Kash. Isn't that what you said earlier?" she asked, but he didn't respond. He was too busy licking her neck. "Do I need to quote your words?"

"Yeah, quote them." He pulled the straps to her neon green bra down. He kissed the top of her left breast before drawing circles with his tongue.

"Stop so I can remind you, Kash." Her voice echoed in the huge space.

He kept his lips on her breast. Only moving his eyes up to look at her, he watched her head tilt back to the glass and her eyes close.

"Remind me."

"You said," she began, and he whipped her entire left breast out. "Girl, ain't nobody..." She stopped talking and moaned as he sucked her nipple and pulled her panties down a little past her hips.

"Mmhmm." Although he was all over her, being

very attentive to her body, he was listening.

"Tryna fuck you." Her moans and southern twang made her words sound sexy.

Kash took her breast from his mouth and stood up.

"Why did you stop?"

"I'm not tryna fuck you." He pulled her bra straps and panties back up. He wanted to see how far she would let him go. "But I could if I wanted to. I don't want you to be that type of woman, giving me you without me giving you me completely. Don't give me that much power." Although his dick was like a brick right now, he didn't want to sex Heaven and then go lay up with Asia. She meant so much more than that to him.

"Kashmir." She rolled her eyes and flared her nostrils. "What are you doing?"

He kissed her forehead and stepped back. "Its Killa K, and I'ma hit your line tomorrow to check on you." He began to walk from the bathroom.

"What the hell just happened?" she whispered to herself before standing from the glass and following behind Kash. "Wait, where are you going?"

"I'm going home. I gotta call Dre and let him know you're good," he said to her over his shoulder.

She shook her head; she was confused as hell. What

the hell went left that damn quick?

"I will talk to you tomorrow then," she said as they reached the front door.

"Can we meet up at the park? I would love to hear Kamelia's voice." He turned to look at her.

"Yeah, of course. I can call her for you." A grimace was on Heaven's face as she tucked her hair behind her ears. She was still confused.

"Cool." He hugged her tightly before opening the door and walking out.

FIVE

Pretty brown eyes, you know I see you.

it's a disguise the way you treat me.

You keep holding on to your thoughts of rejection.

If you with me, you're secure.

Kash pulled up to the forest preserve, in his 2019 Chevrolet Camaro, with Pretty Brown Eyes by Mint Condition softly playing in the background. He parked in the lot, let his windows down, killed the engine, and picked up the bag he had sitting on the passenger seat. Inside the bag held a fifth of Don Julio tequila, lime juice, and a plastic cup. His mind was running crazy with thoughts of Asia and Heaven. He compared the two. Which woman would be perfect for him? They both seemed to have toxic ways, but he knew Heaven's disdain for him stemmed from his absence in

Kamelia's life. But he wasn't willing to take the full blame for that. Both he and Heaven played a role in him not being there. Still, he compared Heaven and Asia as women and mothers.

Truthfully, he didn't really know what type of woman Heaven was because he hadn't seen her in years; however, he remembered who she was back in the day - a beautiful girl with a beautiful soul. Her bubbly personality was what attracted him to her in the first place, and it bewildered him how, even though she hated him, her light still seemed to shine. She didn't let their past affect the way she cared for herself. She still carried herself well. She was still beautiful. She had her own, and she didn't need him. Although her love for him was still obvious, he loved the way she tried to protect herself and her feelings from him. She didn't come off as desperate or needy, and that shit was sexy as hell. He wanted her in every way imaginable, but he didn't want to come back into her life just to hurt her all over again. He asked her if they could start over because he wanted to make things right, but he knew he couldn't step into this with Asia riding his coattail. He had to break things off with her, and he had to do it tonight.

Popping the cork to the bottle, he opted out of pouring a cup. Instead, he put the bottle to his mouth and drank it as if it was ice cold water. He was ready to be with the right woman if Heaven would have him.

It was true that he didn't love Asia. He never tried

to. She was just someone to pass the time with. With her, he felt like he was sleeping with a psychopath. She was a tainted soul. Her vibration was a little off. She was a little too toxic, and she took her pain out on her three helpless children. Yeah, she was a beautiful woman, but she didn't have any substance. She didn't know her own worth. She thought that pussy and pushing out babies for a man would keep him around. She thought a man was all she needed to maintain functionality, regardless of how he treated her. She was very insecure and unable to stand on her own.

Honestly, Kash didn't want his woman to work, but she had to bring something to the table, even if that was only a good, genuine heart and a beautiful attitude that didn't nag or stress him out. His life outside of home was crazy enough. When he was home with his family, he wanted to feel appreciated.

Kash had dealt with Asia for months, fucking her and purposely giving her the bare minimum, the same shit he would give any bitch on the street because he didn't really want to build any longevity with her.

After killing Agents Bullock and Hassan, Dre made sure Kash banked a million. Kash could've given Asia the world. She wouldn't have to worry about a car note or her deadbeat baby daddies. He had the money to hold her down, but every day, she proved to him she wasn't worthy of him.

Asia had nothing to offer in return, not even a home

cooked meal. She was willing to give him pussy whenever he wanted it, but that wasn't enough to keep him, especially since she continuously pushed the issue about not wanting him to use condoms with her. He knew she was trying to trap him the same way she purposely tried to trap her three baby daddies. However, Kash wasn't going in her raw. The fact of the matter was he wasn't going in anybody raw. Pussy and head came a dime a dozen, and although her sex was good, it wasn't good enough to keep him. He could honestly get that from anywhere.

The only thing that kept him around was his attachment to her kids. It fucked him up to witness the way she treated them, and he knew that if he wasn't there, she would eventually lose it and hurt them. He felt terrible even dealing with a woman as broken as Asia because she was who his mother used to be.

Kash laid his seat back and just chilled, vibing to the classic R&B music as it played softly in his ears. With one hand propped behind his head and the other hand babysitting his liquor, he was lost in his thoughts. His heart urged him to consider pursuing his past. He needed to see where things with him and Heaven would go, but his mind told him to protect those babies from Asia and her fucked up ways. Still, that was not his responsibility. He had his own daughter to raise, and Heaven was here, giving him that opportunity.

He took another swallow from his bottle, watching from his rearview mirror as the headlights of a silver

Toyota Camry shook him from his thoughts. The car looked familiar, but for his safety, he pulled his gun from his waist and sat his seat back up. The car pulled up on the side of him with the windows down, and he smiled.

"What you doing out this late?" he asked. He opened his driver's door and climbed out with his bottle still in one hand and his gun in the other. He walked over to Nadia's car, opened the passenger's door, and took a seat.

Kash and Nadia were like best friends. She knew him like the back of her hand. When he left Heaven's apartment, he stood at her door for at least five minutes, debating on if he should go back inside. While standing there, he texted Nadia and told her what had just happened between him and Heaven. She told him not to lead Heaven on. She told him to just go home and sleep on it, and if he still felt the same way in the morning, break things off with Asia and go get his woman.

So, he left, but he wasn't going home to think these thoughts. Instead, he came to the one place where he allowed his thoughts to roam freely. The quietness of the night, the warm breezy air wiping past his face, and the sight of nature and all its calmness always helped his mind go to war.

"Boy," Nadia yawned, "you woke me up out my sleep. Heaven need to take her ass back to Atlanta because this is not like you. Are you okay?" She sat there with a Nike hat on her head, pulled down low, a pair of spandex shorts, and a Nike sweatshirt zipped all the way up to her chin.

"My bad, cuz. I didn't know you was gon' come tracking me down this late at night."

"Yeah, yeah, nigga. You knew I was gon' come see about you. Your text messages seemed kinda urgent."

"Man, Nadia," Kash said and slowly shook his head.

"You're in love, cousin. I can see it written all over your face. I read it in your text. Since when do you text me, asking if you should fuck a female or not?"

"I wouldn't say I'm in love, but I can see myself loving her. I just wanna handle her with care. You know what I'm saying? I don't want to do her dirty. She's dealt with enough of my shit."

"Awwww, Kashmir, you're making my heart swoon." She laughed. "No, but seriously, you need to tell both Asia and Heaven how you feel. You deserve to be happy."

"Yeah, I plan to talk to them both. I had to come out here and get my thoughts together first because Asia been acting crazy as hell."

"Uh oh! Pass me that bottle first." Nadia laughed,

but she was serious. He passed the bottle to her, and she held her hand up, shushing Kash as she drank a long swallow.

"Yeah, you're gonna need it."

"Okay, I'm ready." She passed the bottle back.

"Heaven showed me a picture Asia posted on social media of me, her, and her kids looking like a big, happy ass family. Imagine how that made Heaven feel. Seeing me play daddy when I'm not even being a father to our daughter," he said. "G, I don't even have a Facebook, Instagram, or none of that shit. But mafuckas feel like it's cool to post me. I got rid of social media for that purpose alone."

"Maybe she felt like it was okay because y'all are in a relationship."

"Man, fuck that. We are - well, we were - dating. That shit is over now."

"Damn. That was quick."

"That's not all, G. Earlier, before I left Asia's house, we got into this heated argument about me fucking Heaven and me not loving her. I can admit that I showed my ass over Heaven in front of Asia on the block. I tried to break Esha's truck window because Heaven wouldn't talk to me. Before I left Heaven's crib, I shot a hole in her bathroom door because she said she had a nigga in there," he said, and Nadia sat back, listening. "Man, what the fuck is wrong with me?"

"Damn, Kash. That young girl got you acting like that?"

"I guess. But after me and Asia's little argument, she started talking about she won't be able to live without me. Those words sent a fucking chill down my spine. Honestly, she scared the fuck outta me."

"So, is she threatening to kill herself if you leave her?"

"That's what I took from it. I could be trippin' though. I ain't never had a bitch that was ready to die for the dick."

"Silly… Don't let her stop you from walking away from her, baby cuz. I am rooting for you and Heaven. That Asia girl is nuts." Nadia continued to talk, giving Kash her honest opinion while he drowned himself in Don Julio. "So, go to Asia and tell her 'Bitch, its over', and then go back to Heaven's apartment and do what you feel is best. But don't have sex with her tonight. That'll be a little too much for both of you guys emotionally. Y'all need to hangout, get to know each other, and start a friendship. Be open and honest with her. Encourage her to be the same way with you. Between me and you, cousin, us women dream of marrying a man who we can call our lover and best friend. Real love is about more than just sex."

"Thank you, cuz. I needed to hear that."

"No problem. You know your big cousin got your back. Now, let me get another shot of that liquor." He passed the bottle back to her.

"I thought you said tequila was nasty?" Grinning, he opened the door and stepped out.

"No, I said Patron is nasty... Here." After closing the door, Kash reached inside and took the bottle from her hand. He put it to his lips and tilted it. "Kash, is it that serious?"

"Hell yeah. Buddy ain't working with a full deck. She probably gon' stab my ass."

"I'm about to follow you to her house. I'ma beat her ass if she put her hands on you."

"Naw, cuz. I'm just fucking around. But I'ma get up with you later. Get home safe."

"You too. Call me when you're done with Asia. Are you going to see Heaven afterwards?"

"Probably. I'll call you." He walked over to his car and got in. As Nadia backed out of her parking spot, Kash started up his engine. He reversed out his spot, and after that, he sped away.

It was about 2:15 a.m. when he stepped up to Asia's front door and knocked. He still had the bottle of Don Julio in his hand as he heard the door unlock and open slightly.

"Asia," Kash said, opening the door all the way. He watched as Asia began to walk away. "Asia!"

"Kash, get in here. Why are you standing outside, calling my name?"

He didn't want to go inside because he didn't plan to be there long. He just wanted to break things off with Asia as quickly as possible.

"I need to go, but I have to talk to you first."

"What's up?" Asia walked back to the door and stood there. The smell of Heaven's perfume wafted up her nose, causing her to step closer to Kash and sniff his shirt.

"Where did you just come from?" she asked. "Were you with another bitch?" Kash licked his lips and sat down on the porch's banister.

"I was with Heaven," he said honestly.

"You were with who?" she asked before stepping into his face and slapping him. Instantly, his right cheek began to turn red. He stayed seated as he moved his head, frowned, and grabbed her hands, holding them in place. "Let me go, Kash."

"Listen to me," he said. "I let you slide with the first slap. Don't let that shit happen again." He pushed her back by her arms. He understood her being upset, but he didn't play that touchy feely shit. And he didn't fight women.

"Why did you even come back over here, Kash? I mean, God, you leave from fucking her, just to come over here and throw it in my face," she cried.

"I don't know why the fuck I'm here besides me feeling like I owe you an explanation," he said, squinting. "But honestly, I've given yo' ungrateful ass enough of me. I don't owe you shit. Then, you go on Instagram and post my business. Creating this fake ass happy family persona. That picture you posted was fuckery at its finest. I left here earlier, feeling bad about how I made you feel on the block earlier, but then I stumble across a picture of me and thought you gotta be one desperate bitch." Kash stood up. "I'm done fucking with you."

"Kash." She grabbed his arm. "I didn't think it would be a problem. But I can delete the picture if you want me to. Just please don't leave."

"It's too late. Save your memories and your tears, Asia." He walked down the steps, leaving Asia on the porch alone, crying. On his way to his car, he took a sip from his bottle. And just like that, he and Asia were over. He knew his reasoning was lame; however, he wanted out. Heaven was here, and he wasn't letting her go.

Thirty minutes later, he was climbing into bed, half naked, behind a sleeping Heaven. He snuggled up against her, spooning her. He kissed her neck before laying his head on the pillow and falling into a deep sleep.

The next morning, when Heaven turned over, she screamed, scared out of her mind. Before she went to bed, no one was there, and she remembered locking her door. She had no clue how Kash got in.

"Kash, how did you get in here?"

"Shhh, lay down. Your breath stink, ma, while you screaming all in my face and shit. I used your spare key."

"Remind me to find it and move it," she said as Kash grabbed her and pulled her to him.

"Man, you ain't moving shit. Lay the fuck down."

Heaven laid her head on his chest, and he rubbed her back. She was completely naked, but she felt comfortable being bare in front of him.

"Yeah, okay," she said, kissing his chest. She looked up at him and stared into his face. His eyes were closed, and his lips were open slightly, so she put her index finger in his mouth, and he sucked it.

"Why are you staring at me?"

"I don't know. You somehow suckered your way back into my life."

"You a sucker for love, shorty?"

"Love? Who said I love you?"

"You haven't said it yet, but I know that's how you feel."

"You just look so much like Kamelia. I want you to meet her," she said, getting off the subject. Her heart was racing, and her nerves were getting the best of her.

"I like how you switched the conversations. But shit, let's go get her and bring her here."

"Can we give it a few weeks? I think we need to date and get to know each other first. I know she's your daughter and all, but like you said, let's start over."

"That's cool." He opened his eyes and looked at her. Sitting up slightly, he kissed her lips. Now that things were over between him and Asia, he was about to give Heaven his all. At least he planned to.

"We can go down to Atlanta, and you can meet my father too."

"So, I need his approval to be a father to my daughter?"

"Hell naw, but my father's opinion and blessings mean a lot to me."

"Aight." Kash closed his eyes and held Heaven close to him. He was willing to take a trip to Atlanta.

He could appreciate how she looked to her father for guidance, and he prayed that one day soon, he and Kamelia would have that same relationship.

Heaven put her hand under the covers and ran her fingers across Kash's morning erection. She wondered if sex with Kash still felt the same after all these years. Kissing his chest, Heaven took control of him, and for the rest of the morning, they went at it like two dogs in heat.

SIX

"Jayla, Marie, are y'all there?" Reign asked.

"Yes, friend," Jayla said. "I just merged Marie in."

"Yes, my love. I'm here. What's goody, lil' ladies?" Marie announced herself.

"I got so much shit going on out here. I just really need a listening ear, but I know you hoes gon' have your opinions."

"Now you know that just a listening ear shit is dead, Reign." Jayla said.

Reign sucked her teeth. "I know, Jayla. That's why I said what I said. I swear I need a new set of friends."

"Like who? Yo 'dry, scary ass sister, Denim?" Marie asked. "Bitch, please. The way she stood there while you and Anika fought. That bitch didn't even get out the pool."

"Biiiiittch!" Jayla exclaimed. "I was just thinking

about that. Heaven told us everything. I wanted to get in that bitch's ass, but you handled yourself, sis."

"I didn't need Denim's help. Anika play that crazy role, and they say crazy people can fight, but these hands here are compliments of Montae Jackson."

"Well, who is Denim's hands compliments of? Her pussy ass," Jayla said, laughing.

"Girl, fuck y'all. This phone call has a purpose. I didn't call to talk about Denim." The phone went silent with Jayla and Marie awaiting what this phone call was about. "I'm not really good at keeping secrets, y'all."

"No shit, bitch." Marie laughed. "None of us are."

"Right," Jayla agreed.

"No, seriously. I got some shit on me, and I cannot hold this shit in no more."

"Girl!" Jayla yelled. "You are so annoying. My pregnant body can't take anticipation. Just say the shit."

"Let me guess first," Marie said. "Sno made you and Anika apologize. Afterwards, y'all had a threesome. You ate her pussy, she ate your ass, and now Sno is a happy man."

"No, you nasty ass freak. Sno can't make me do shit. I'm not eating no coochie, and Anika can kiss my ass."

"Damn, that would've been some great gossip," Marie whispered.

"I hate you. I'm so sorry to disappoint you, Marie, but the reason for this phone call is to tell y'all that Delilah isn't Demarco's daughter."

"Bitch, what?" Marie and Jayla yelled in unison.

"You are lying, Reign," Marie said.

"Marie don't start calling people liars. I can believe it. Delilah don't look shit like the rest of them kids. Hell, Kamelia look more like Sno than Delilah, and that's only his granddaughter. Ugh, Anika is so fucking triflin' with her bitch ass."

"Yes, Heaven said Anika has been taking Delilah up to this prison, that I am sitting in the parking lot of right now, to see this nigga everybody calls Bully. He's claiming that he is her real daddy."

"So, you on some real investigators type of shit right now?" Marie asked.

"Yes, this bitch done caused years of havoc in our lives and marriage. It is time to cut her ass off. Now, although I really, really hate that bitch's guts, I don't want to hurt Demarco or betray Heaven's trust. I told Heaven I wouldn't say anything until it was the right time," Reign said into the receiver as she sat in her car. She was outside of Dooly State Prison in Unadilla, Georgia, an hour and thirty minutes south of Atlanta.

"Well, when will the time be right? Because I'm ready to see how this shit unfolds. My pregnant ass ain't had no drama in a hot little minute. Shit, I think I'm going through withdrawals."

"You took the words right outta my mouth," Marie said.

"Initially, I was going to break it to him gently, and then I was going to pass him my ultrasounds and say 'Congratulations, baby, we are expecting twins.' But my big belly revealed itself before I could say anything."

"Okay, so I have a dumb question."

"You always have a slow ass question, Marie."

"She's just a little special. Marie, me and Reign don't have time for your simpleminded questions."

"No, y'all. It's a good dumb question." Marie laughed. Jayla and Reign had a habit of ganging up on her.

"Go ahead, Marie. Ask your question." Reign laughed.

"What are you doing up at the prison?"

"Marie, I'm here to see this shit with my own eyes." Reign broke down the entire situation to her friends. "After Heaven told me this nigga's name, I searched for him on the DCOR website. That's

Georgia's correctional website," she said before Marie could ask another dumb question. "About three men popped up with his name. Bitch, I wrote all three of they asses. I didn't know how he looked, and the pictures they had on the website didn't give me any clues of who the real Bully was. I put my phone number on the letter and told them to call me." Reign laughed. "I got a response from only one of them last week. He called me while I was having breakfast with the family at KeKe and King's house."

"Bittttch!" Jayla said, gasping.

"I know, right. But I had to take that call. So, I politely excused myself from the table and ran my ass to the bathroom. He told me he is in fact Delilah's father. He didn't know anything about Demarco being a possibility. He said Anika told him she was no longer messing around with my husband at the time. The dude, Bully, has been locked up since Anika was about four months pregnant. That's why it was so easy for her to put Delilah off on Demarco. At first, Bully didn't want Anika to bring Delilah up to the prison. Y'all know the usual story. He didn't want her to see her father locked up, but recently, he was diagnosed with some type of bacterial meningitis on his brain."

"Meningitis? That ain't no life-threatening disease. His dumb ass. He must have some fucked up ass breath though," Marie stated seriously.

"Huh?" Reign asked. A grimaced expression was

apparent in her tone.

"Doesn't meningitis cause stinky breath?" Marie asked seriously.

"Bitch!" Jayla hollered. "That's gingivitis. You damn fool."

"Marie," Reign smirked, "you gotta stop acting like your parents didn't pay for you to get a good education. Like seriously."

"Reign and Jayla, go to hell, okay? Respectfully."

"Anyways, I don't really know shit about the infection, nor do I care, but he claimed he was given a year to live. So, he wanted to meet his daughter and spend time with her before he dies. He told me the days Anika usually brings Delilah up here, so here I am."

Jayla and Marie were silent as Reign spilled all the tea. They all knew this day was coming soon. Anika was one deceitful ass bitch who used her kids as a weapon against the only man who was willing to deal with her bullshit. Delilah's paternity had always been in question, and now, Reign was close to getting rid of Anika forever. Although Sno and Anika would still have a kid in common, Heaven was an adult. She couldn't use her to make Sno bow down to her demands. In a few weeks, this shit would either be a wrap or the paternity test would come back and tie Sno and Anika for another nine years.

"I been sitting on this shit for two weeks now."

Reign loved Delilah, but she couldn't front. She prayed the paternity came back in Bully's favor. She knew Sno would be hurt, but with time, he would get over it.

"So, what are you planning to do as far as the paternity test? Are you about to go in there and swab him?"

"Now, how in the hell is she about to go swab him, Marie? She ain't no damn lawyer or court official."

"Jayla, shut the hell up. I thought maybe she got clearance or something."

"Girl," Jayla sighed, muttering, "Marie, please just hush."

"No, I contacted the Paternity Court show. Bully will be tested soon. Now, all I have left to do is tell Demarco. I'm waiting for Anika and Delilah to come from the building, so I can FaceTime him."

"That's how you're going to break the news to him?"

"Yes."

"That just seems so coldhearted."

"I know, but he has to find out one way or another. And this is the best way."

After Reign's conversation with Jayla and Marie, she FaceTimed Sno. She was silent as she pointed the camera in the direction of the building.

"Reign, what you doing at a prison?" Sno asked. Still, she didn't say anything.

She slid down in her seat as she saw Anika and Delilah enter the parking lot. She followed them with her camera. At this point, Sno was also quiet. With tears in her eyes, Reign stared at Sno's face as he looked confused at the entire ordeal. Delilah yanked her hand away from Anika's and swung the back door open before getting inside and slamming it.

"Is this real?" he asked.

"Yes," Reign finally said. "I didn't know how else to tell you without having proof, but Delilah isn't your daughter." She turned the camera around. "Her father is a man named Donterio Brown. I've talked to him, and he told me everything. I'm sorry, baby."

Sno closed his eyes and hung his head while sighing. In that moment, Reign wanted to run to him to comfort him. This news had to be breaking his heart. Her bottom lip was poked out as she looked at him. He wasn't afraid to cry in front of her. Seeing as though not one tear fell from his eyes, she knew a part of him was upset, but another part of him was relieved.

"What do you want me to do? Do you need to talk to Anika? I can go over there and give her the phone."

"Nah, don't give her shit. I'm not worried about it."

"Are you sure? You don't deserve this bullshit, Demarco."

"Reign, I'm good. I don't want you around Anika. You're pregnant. I don't want y'all fighting. This is my bullshit to handle."

"Okay," Reign said shortly.

"How did you know about this?" The top of Sno's head came into view as he scratched his head.

He looked back up at Reign as she said, "Delilah told Heaven. Before you get upset with Heaven, I told her not to tell you and promised her I wouldn't say anything to you either until I had facts."

"Delilah telling Heaven was facts enough, Reign!" He yelled, and Reign jumped. "Look, I didn't mean to scream at you. I'm sorry."

"I know, and I'm sorry I kept this from you. I just didn't want you to be sad. With me being pregnant with the twins…"

"You kept that shit from me too."

"Baby, I know. I just didn't want either thing to overshadow the other. I love you, Demarco."

"I love you too, Reign. I'm good, mane. I want a paternity test though."

"I'm on it," Reign said. She was so nervous as she spoke to him. She was afraid of what he was going to do to Anika and what this meant for their relationship with Delilah.

"I'ma break that bitch neck when I see her. I'm supposed to get Delilah today, but I'ma cancel," he sighed. "I can't be around her right now. I don't want to treat her differently. I would rather get my emotions together."

"I understand, bae."

"Reign, just get home. I can't be here alone right now. I need to rub on your stomach."

"I'm on my way."

SEVEN

The morning Kash and Heaven had sex, Heaven decided she needed time to herself. She needed to get her thoughts together before taking things further. Although Kash had just broken things off with Asia, Heaven didn't want to rush into anything with Kash, and that was because she was still engaged. Plus, she didn't want to complicate things or allow sex to cloud her judgement.

For those reasons, Heaven and Kash hadn't seen each other since that day, but they found themselves talking on the phone every morning, noon, and night like they were teenagers in love, laying up on the phone for hours, getting to know each other. He would ask her to kick it with him, but she would turn him down, knowing that them hanging out would only lead to more sex. Still, she knew he was tired of the distance.

Standing in the kitchen, washing out a bowl and

spoon she'd just used, she sighed and wiped her forehead. Honestly, she was tired of the distance too. He was the whole reason she was here to begin with, but they had barely seen one another. The phone calls were cool, but she could've stayed in Atlanta if all they were going to do was talk on the phone. She wanted to tell him they needed to link up, but she didn't want to come off as crazy or indecisive since them being apart was her idea to being with. Her heart was full of games when it came to Kash, and that was because she didn't know how to be when it came to him.

Just like clockwork, her cell began to ring, and she knew exactly who it was. Running from the kitchen to her bedroom, she picked up her phone, flopped down on her bed, and rolled her eyes. She didn't really feel like talking, but she answered anyway. "Hey, Kashmir." Her voice was dry and uninterested.

"What's up, baby?" he replied, causing her to smile. This was the first time he called her by that name.

"If you're calling to just talk on the phone, you can hang up right now." She poked her bottom lip out.

"Why would I do that? What's your problem? Did I do something?"

"You didn't do anything. I'm tired of just talking on the phone though. I haven't seen you since the day we had sex. It's been two damn weeks. This shit just feels so familiar, minus the swollen feet and morning sickness."

"You told me you needed time, and I've been trying to give you that."

"Kash," she sighed. "Why would you even agree to giving me time? You're leaving room for doubts within me."

"Because you said you needed time to figure out what we were doing. I don't want to rush you."

"Well, what are we doing, Kashmir?"

"We're dating and finding our way to love. I need you," he said honestly. "I haven't went anywhere, and I'm not going anywhere far, baby. You stuck with a nigga for life. If not as your man or husband, I'm here as your friend. So, whatever that familiar shit is you're talking about, you can cancel it. You told me to stay away from you, and I just went along with it."

"What the fuck ever, Kash. If you was really tryna fuck wit' me, you would have ever agreed to that shit."

"What part of I don't want to rush you don't you understand?"

"Whatever, Kashmir."

"Man, fix your fucking attitude. I was actually calling to tell you to get dressed. I'm about to come get you. I have a basketball game, and I need you in the stands, cheering for me."

"Kash, stop lying. You was not going to invite me outside at first. You was calling to cake up on the phone. Now, you wanna be my friend because I have an attitude."

Kash laughed. "G, you think I give a fuck about your attitude?"

"You better give a fuck about my attitude."

"Well, I don't. So, fuck yo' lil' funky ass attitude. And I'm not asking do you want to come outside. I'm telling you that you're coming outside. Be yo' lil' pretty ass ready in about an hour." He hung up.

Heaven took the phone from her ear and just stared at it. She let out an irritated breath. She was appalled. Who the hell did he think he was hanging up on? It was still early in the morning, 7:20 a.m. to be exact, way too early for Kash's demanding attitude, and Heaven wasn't going anywhere with him.

Standing from her bed, she walked to the living room and sat down on her sectional. She snuggled up with a pillow and laid down. Making herself comfortable, she turned the television on, along with her surround sounds, and turned it to a music video channel. As she laid out on her back, she unlocked her phone and scrolled through it. She clicked on her Safari app. Snapping her fingers to the song while typing in Hermes, she searched for a vintage style clutch. After twenty minutes of searching and coming up empty, she laid her phone on her chest and closed her eyes.

Ding! Heaven opened her eyes and looked at her phone.

Esha: Good morning, Sweet Pea.

Heaven: Not Sweet Pea. LOL. Good morning, Esha.

Esha: Are you going to the basketball game?

Heaven: Hell Nah. Did Kash tell you to text me?

Esha: Girl, no.

Heaven: Yea right. Esha, stop lying.

Esha: I'm serious.

Heaven: Well, I guess I will go.

She sat up off the couch and stretched. It was almost eight o'clock. She stood up and walked to her bedroom. She went into her closet and grimaced at all the designer dresses she had hanging up.

"What the hell am I supposed to wear to a basketball game?" From the middle of her closet, she pushed the hangers to the side and heard a clinking noise as her engagement ring hit the floor. She squatted down and picked it up. Examining it, she exhaled. She had forgotten all about it. The night that Kash came to her apartment, she had it on her finger. She wasn't sure if he had seen it or not, but he hadn't said anything to her about it. She couldn't believe how she cried over Kash while wearing Derrick's ring. So, she took it off after Kash left.

When she stood back up, she saw a pretty black, fitted, long, tube top dress that would go perfect with either a pair of jeweled sandals or a pair of Jacquemus black mules she had on her shelf.

Heaven took the dress from inside and laid it out on the bed. She walked back over to the closet and pulled out a cute little wooden stool. Standing on it, she pulled the Jacquemus shoe box down from the shelf and looked inside. Lifting a pair of black shearling, open toe, high heeled mules from the box, she threw her engagement ring inside and closed the lid.

"What you doing?" Heaven jumped and screamed from the sound of Kash's voice coming from behind her. He lifted her from the stool with the shoe box still in her hands. She prayed he didn't make the ring fall out. Softly placing her down onto the bed, he leaned down over her and kissed her lips.

Gripping his ears and smiling widely, Heaven kissed him back before saying, "I told you to remind me to move that spare key."

"And I told you that you ain't moving shit." He kissed her lips again. His phone began to ring, and he took it out his pocket to look at the caller ID while still holding on to Heaven. His nostrils flared, but he remained calm. He just silenced his phone and put it back into his pocket before focusing his attention back on Heaven. He licked his lips and stared at her.

"That better not be one of your little girlfriends calling you." She sat up on her elbows and poked his forehead.

"Chill out, baby."

"Anyways, what if I had company, Kash? You can't just be coming up in my apartment without calling me first. How would Asia feel about you creeping in your baby mama's crib?" she pondered with one eyebrow cocked.

"I don't know, and I don't give a fuck how Asia would feel. I don't fuck wit' shorty no more," he said. "Why aren't you dressed yet?"

"Because I wasn't going at first. You had a lot of nerve, telling me what I was going to do." She cocked her head to the side, and Kash grinned. He let her go, stood up, and scratched his chin as Heaven sat up and looked at him.

"You wasn't going?" he asked, grabbing her hand and pulling her up from the bed. Kash pulled Heaven to him and hugged her. "You got me fucked up, Heaven."

"No, you had me fucked up. You better be lucky

Esha texted me because I was definitely about to take a nap on your ass." She looked up at him and pulled his face to hers.

She couldn't lie. She missed him; she was happy to see him. And although she said she wasn't going, she was really waiting for him to beg or force her to go. Passionately, she kissed him. Her eyes were still wide open as she watched his expression. He closed his eyes as he took her bottom lip into his mouth.

Both breathing heavily, they took in one another's energy as her soft lips caressed his. Moaning, it was clear they missed one another's touch. The feel of his penis up against her, through his basketball shorts, had her thinking about getting on her knees and giving him the best head he'd ever had.

"Do you wanna take a shower with me?" Heaven whispered, her lips still pressed to his.

"Nah, G. You tryna get in my drawers." He chuckled.

"Funny." Pulling away from Kash's grasp, she walked over to her dresser and looked at herself in the mirror. Picking up a necklace, she put it to her neck as she looked at Kash's reflection as he still stood in place.

"We don't have time, lil' freaky ass girl." He walked up behind her and leaned up against her with his chin on the top of her head. He looked at her and then himself as they stood there together. They looked perfect. She was a beautiful woman, and he was a handsome man, and their chemistry was out of this world. He knew how to make her smile when she didn't want to. Somehow, being around her made him feel like she was who he had been missing all these years to make his life complete.

Now, he was ready to meet his daughter. He knew she had to be just as beautiful and perfect in person as she was in the pictures he had in his phone. He often wondered if she had any of his traits, or was she one hundred percent prissy and feisty like Heaven?

"I'm not a freak, Kash. I'm only asking for an innocent shower." She bit her inner cheek. Removing her bonnet from her head, she let all thirty inches of her weave flow down to her ass.

"Nah, G, I already took a shower this morning."

"You smell good too, but Kashmir…" She turned to look at him. She batted her eyes rapidly and pouted her lips. "Please."

"Nah, man. We gotta go."

"It's only a shower." She reiterated. "You acting like I'm tryna fuck you."

He laughed. "Oh! Well, if we not fucking, I'm definitely not getting in the shower with you."

"Kash, fuck you," she exclaimed. When she turned

back around, he wrapped his arms around her. "Move. Get the hell off me. I'm sitting here, begging you to take a shower with me, like I'm a desperate ass bitch." She pushed at his dick with her ass.

"Man, you trippin'." Kash stepped back and took a seat on her bed. He watched her as she walked from the bedroom with an attitude. "I don't need you to fuck me, Kash."

Kash chuckled and stood up. He walked behind her, catching up to her in the hallway. He grabbed her arm. "What I tell you to call me?" He turned her around. Lifting her up off her feet, he wrapped her legs around his waist as she wrapped her arms around his neck.

"I'm not calling you no damn Killa K."

"You will soon enough."

"Yeah, okay." Her tone was condescending as she rolled her eyes.

"You need to fix that fucking attitude." He put his face into the crook of her neck and kissed her.

"I don't have an attitude," she said softly. She put her hands to the back of his head. Putting her fingers in Kash's hair, Heaven massaged his scalp and put her forehead to his. "I thought we had to go?" she asked.

"We do." He put her down and followed her as she

went into the bathroom. Heaven slowly removed her pajama shorts, along with her underwear, and then her top. She looked as if she was trying to seduce him. Kash just stood there in a trance, watching her. The way she took her clothes off while she stared at him put him in deep thought.

"Why are you just standing there, looking at me like that?" she asked, and he smirked.

"I'm just enjoying the show," he said honestly.

"What show?" She turned around, showing Kash her backside as she picked up her shower cap from the sink.

"That show," he replied. She turned back around to look at him.

At this point, his eyes weren't focused on her face. Instead, he looked from her breasts to her privacy. Her ample breasts, flat stomach, curvaceous hips, and shaved vagina were mesmerizing.

"Boy," she said, placing her shower cap on her head and rolling her eyes. She cocked her head to the side.

"I thought you said we have to go?" She reminded himagain.

"We do." Still, he walked over to her.

"Then get out, silly, and let me get ready." She giggled.

Instead of responding, he wrapped one arm around her waist, and with his other hand, he put it around her neck, grabbing her softly. With the knuckle of his index finger, Kash tilted Heaven's face to the side and licked her jawbone before pressing his lips to it and sucking her as she put her hands inside his shirt and rubbed his back.

With her hands and fingers softly gliding up and down his spine, Kash instantly caught chills all over his body. So, he decided he would take her up on that take a shower offer, praying that whatever they decided to do wouldn't fuck up his ability to still show up and show out on the court. Honestly, he couldn't really think about anything besides being inside Heaven. Right now, basketball was the furthest thing from his mind. With her hands still caressing his back, Kash pulled away from Heaven long enough to pull his shirt over his head. Tossing it, his shirt landed on the floor, next to their feet.

This is what Heaven didn't want. Every time they came around each other, they were in full lust mode. But at the same time, this was what she wanted. Kash was who she needed.

As he began to come out of his shoes, socks, shorts, and then boxers, Heaven stood on her toes and walked over to the shower. Upon reaching the shower door, she looked back at Kash and winked her eye before stepping inside.

He was on her heels. He walked over, dick erect and standing at attention. He stepped in behind her and closed the glass door. He stood behind her. Bending down slightly, he put his face into the crook of her neck as she turned the shower on.

"Argh!" Screaming and jumping back from the few drops of cold water that hit her body, she hit Kash in his face with the back of her head.

"Shit," he said, moving back against the wall. He put his hand to his nose, closed his eyes, and leaned his head back.

"I'm so sorry." Turning on her heels, she wrapped her arms around him. "Let me see." Pulling at his arm and cupping his face, she examined him. She ran her fingers over his nose. "You're okay. It's not broken."

"I know wit' yo' big head, dramatic ass. The water wasn't that cold."

"Boy, shush!" Heaven put her fingernail to his lips, and he kissed her finger while looking her in her eyes. As the water poured down on the two, Heaven kissed Kash from his neck to his chest. She kept her finger on his lips. Trailing her tongue from his chest to his abs, she left behind soft kisses as she made her way down.

Kash was silent with his eyes on her and his bottom lip trapped in between his teeth. The further down she went, the harder he bit down on his bottom lip. Anticipation caused his teeth to clamp down and his body to tremble. This couldn't be the same sweet Heaven who was afraid to get her pussy ate a few years back. Nah, this couldn't be the same Heaven who was soft spoken and timid. This definitely wasn't the Heaven from five years ago because, back then, she didn't know how to take dick. She didn't know what to do with it. She didn't know how to receive pleasure, and she damn sure didn't know how to give it. Now, she knew exactly what to do with it. Now, she knew how to intrigue and please a man.

Squatting, Heaven took her time licking and kissing Kash's swollen manhood. She slowly took him in, inch by inch, swallowing him and damn near making his entire dick disappear, causing Kash to close his eyes and lean his head up against the wall. Heaven had her head game down pact. Kash wasn't a small man, but Heaven was handling him like he was a lil' nigga. She had him moaning, grabbing at her wig, and climbing the walls, showing him she was a grown ass woman.

Shooing his hand from her hair, she held his pole with one hand while her other hand was against his chest.

"Fuck," he moaned. "Heaven." Her name rolled off his tongue lustfully. Adrenaline rushed his body, making his heart beat rapidly. He couldn't hold back any longer. He climaxed in her mouth. And of course, she swallowed it all.

She stood up and wiped the water from her eyes,

kissing his chest. Kash grabbed her by her hand and turned her around before bending her over. Now, it was his turn to please her. Breaking his number one rule of not having unprotected sex with anyone, he took his time entering her, thrusting slowly. He could've easily been mistaken as a stripper. His strokes were slow yet powerful. They were precise, strong, and full of passion. It was as if he was in a trance.

"Killa K," she yelled. This was what she meant. This was how she wanted to be fucked, and Derrick could never. The way Kash was making her feel, the way he had her back arched while she screamed for mercy, she called him Killa K because Kash was definitely killing her insides. The way he kept her body under his control, the way he rubbed her back, ass, and thighs while still rotating his hips showed he wasn't new to this. Stroking Kash's ego, Heaven talked to him while she threw it back.

"Killa," she said as the water ran down her face. "It's over with for that bitch, Asia, and any other bitch you're entertaining."

"Yeah." He moaned back.

"You're mine, and I'm yours."

"Are you sure? Are you ready for me?" he asked. "Are you ready for a relationship?"

"Yes, Killa!" she screamed as he pulled her up by the back of her neck. She was so into the moment that she had forgotten that she was already in a relationship, an engagement to be exact.

"Killa what?" he asked, whispering into her ear.

"K." Somehow, Heaven ended up trapped in between Kash and the wall, being choked and fucked all at the same time. Before she knew it, they both were howling, grunting, and coming to an amazing peak.

EIGHT

After the long morning Kash and Heaven had, he was exhausted, but he still managed to give one hundred fifty percent at the basketball game. The outdoor court was jam packed with men and women spectating as Lance and Kash put in work.

Growing up, sports was all Kash really had. Being an only child to a selfish woman, who spent most of her time up a man's ass in order to provide, Kash was left alone. Raising himself and grooming himself to be the man he was today, he used sports as an outlet and escape. With the right guidance, he could've become something great in life. The entire hood saw the potential in him, but he chose to become a product of his environment.

It seemed as if everyone was outside today. Without a question, they'd come out to watch Kash and Lance effortlessly win their last game for the summer and take home $20,000. If only he would've been this motivated back in the day, he might've had the opportunity to go pro.

As they played, Heaven and Esha were in their own zone. They hadn't seen each other in two weeks, and they hadn't really talked. At first, they were quiet, too quiet. But soon enough, after Esha broke the ice, their conversation began to flow.

Esha was sure Heaven had some juicy gossip to tell her since she was here with Kash at his championship game. The real question was why wasn't Asia here instead? Heaven and Kash had to have made up, and Heaven was holding out on her. She sat staring at Heaven for the longest time, watching her as she watched the game with a smile on her face.

Heaven and Esha looked like two proud girlfriends. They were both dressed up nicely.

Esha was dressed in a pair of blue jean shorts, a yellow Lakers jersey, with a purple tube top underneath, and a pair of long, yellow and purple socks with LA Lakers scripted on the sides. Her shoes were a pair of purple, yellow, and white Jordan 1s, and her hair was box braided. She was dressed for the occasion while Heaven took a different route.

Her blonde wig was bone straight, and the little black dress she found in the back of her closet had her looking snatched. Deciding to go with the Jacquemus heels, she was ready to stand on the side of her man after he won this game. She had a set of diamond studs in her ears and a diamond pendent necklace around her neck. She sat there with a piece of gum in her mouth, obnoxiously chewing and blowing bubbles.

Both women had on big sunglasses that covered their eyes for two different reasons. Esha used hers to shield her eyes from the sun while Heaven's glasses shielded her from Esha's prying eyes. Even through her tints, Heaven could see Esha looking at her from the corner of her eye.

"Sooooo," Esha said, scooting a little closer to Heaven, so they could hear one another while they talked. Smiling at Heaven, Esha playfully pushed her shoulder.

"What?" she asked, keeping her eyes on Kash and the game. She was blushing so hard that she tried not to look at Esha. Heaven knew what Esha's sooooooo was all about, but she was not ready to tell her anything. She was still in the confused stages of her and Kash's relationship, and she didn't want to sound stupid. For one, she put on a big ass show two weeks ago, crying and fussing about how she didn't want Kash to see her. Now, she was sitting here at his basketball game, being all supportive and shit. She just wasn't ready to talk about her and Kash, and she definitely wasn't about to tell Esha how Kash fucked her so good that she asked him to be her man. Although it was in the heat of the moment, she still didn't want to divulge that.

"Don't play wit' me, Heaven. Look at you." Esha smirked, moving Heaven's hair to the side. "You out here with your skin all glowing and shit, looking like a sexy, rich bitch. Kash let you wear this tight ass dress outside?"

"This is a natural glow, friend," she said, still looking straight ahead. She smiled widely, showing every single tooth in her mouth. She briefly looked at Esha. "Girl, Kash can't tell me shit. I am so grown, Esha. You have no idea how much I've grown over these past couple of weeks." She flipped her hair to her back and looked at the game, smirking as she bit down on the side of her bottom lip.

Esha smirked as well, knowing Heaven was full of shit. "Ooouuuu, Heaven Wright, you are so nasty. You and Killa. You freaked him, didn't you?" She squinted her eyes and pursed her lips together.

"Girl, no!"

"Look at me, Heaven," Esha said.

"For what?"

"I want you to tell me that shit with a straight fucking face."

Heaven sucked her teeth and looked at Esha. Esha removed Heaven's glasses.

"Okay, let's try this again." She cleared her throat and repeated herself. "Ooouuuu, Heaven Wright, you are so nasty. You freaked him, didn't you?" The entire time Esha talked, Heaven blushed.

"Girl, no. I didn't freak him, but he fucked me, and I gave him this A1 head," she said, and they both screamed. It was as if everyone stopped doing what they were doing to look in Heaven and Esha's direction.

Cocking her head forward with a stank look on her face, Esha asked, "What the fuck y'all looking at?"

"Y'all loud ass." Somebody in the crowd shouted.

"Shut the fuck up!" Somebody else yelled.

"Bitch, that smart ass mouth about to get us beat up," Heaven said, laughing.

"Tell me about it," Esha said as she looked around at the audience.

"They acting like this a real NBA game."

"I mean, it's the closest thing, and your man is like a celebrity... He is your man, right?"

"Maybe." She took her sunglasses from Esha's hand and put them back on. Turning her head back to the game, both her and Esha sat, cheering their men on.

Suddenly, the crowd in the stands went wild, watching the clock as Lance caught a rebound. He ran down the court with his opponent on his ass. Passing the ball to Kash, he cockily dribbled it in between his legs as the clock counted down. Two seconds before the buzzer sounded, he went up and took the three-point shot that floated through the air before connecting to the top of the rim. The orange basketball swooshed around the rim before falling inside.

It was as if the entire crowd ran out onto the court. They all swarmed around the two men and congratulated them, including three little kids. All of the children looked familiar to Heaven as she and Esha made their way over to their men with serious expressions on their faces.

"Kaaaassshh!" The little ones yelled in unison.

The two little girls clung on to his legs while the little boy reached for Kash to pick him up. Kash had to admit that he had a soft spot for Asia's kids. He had known them for less than a year, but he loved them. As he picked Taiwan up, Heaven walked up to him as Esha walked over to Lance with her hands on her hips.

"This guy." Esha smirked.

"Man, Esha, that's not our business." Lance licked his lips and grabbed Esha around her waist, hugging her as he whispered in her ear. "But I got a feeling shit is about to hit the fan. Those are Asia's kids, so I know she is out here somewhere."

"No shit, Lance. This shit is going to be my business if she comes over here acting crazy." Esha promised.

"Esha, you gotta chill. Let Killa handle his women. That nigga don't fuck with Asia no more."

"Sure!" she said facetiously, kissing his lips before turning around to look at Heaven and Kash.

"Who do we have here?" Heaven asked as if she didn't already know who they were. She cupped Kash's face and pulled him in for a passionate kiss while he still held Asia's son in his arms.

"These are Asia's kids."

"Hey, kids." Heaven put on a phony smile. She knew Asia was somewhere watching, so she had to put on a little show. She'd never been a jealous person. Besides, the kids didn't have anything to do with this. This was between adults. Still, that didn't stop her from being petty. Kneeling, she shook Malaysia and India's hands.

"This is Malaysia and India." Kash introduced as Heaven looked up at him. In his mind, he thought about how secure Heaven had to be. She was gentle and nice to Asia's kids. Most women would have acted an ass in this situation but not Heaven, especially since she was purposely trying to piss Asia off.

"Oh, you two have such beautiful names."

"Thank you," the two girls said, smiling bashfully at Heaven.

"Malaysia and India are the names of countries in Asia. Pretty names for two pretty girls." Heaven smiled. "It was nice meeting you, Malaysia and India."

"What the fuck?" Esha whispered to Lance.

"G, I don't know. Killa must've put that act right on her ass." He shrugged.

"Must have."

Heaven stood and turned to Kash. She smiled at him and pinched Taiwan's chubby cheek. "And what is your name, handsome?"

"His name is Taiwan," Malaysia answered.

"Woooow! Miss Asia is pretty clever with the names," Heaven said as she held her arms out, and Taiwan went to her. She kissed his cheek, put him on her hip, and asked Lance to take a picture of them as she handed him her phone. Kash frowned and so did Lance and Esha. They all looked at her. "What? Come on, let's take a picture with your little fans. Put your arm around my waist, Kash."

Before Lance could take the picture, a loud, boisterous voice rang out through the crowd, causing a scene and bringing a slight smirk to Heaven's lips.

"Kash, what the fuck? Bitch, put my gaddam son down." She walked over, attempting to snatch Taiwan from Heaven, but Kash quickly intervened, grabbing

Asia up before she even had the chance to touch Taiwan.

"Watch it, bitch!" Heaven threatened, laughing. She annunciated every syllable. She wasn't bothered by Asia at all, and her kids were very friendly and respectful.

"You let that bitch touch my kids, Kash?" She swung at him, throwing a few jabs that didn't connect because he blocked them. "You saw me calling you earlier. Why didn't you answer? You don't think you should've told me you were bringing her to your game? That way I wouldn't have showed up and embarrassed myself in front of my kids."

"No, I don't think I should've told you shit, Asia," he said nonchalantly, shrugging his shoulders.

"What the fuck, Kash? You're out here kissing her in public?"

He didn't respond right away. He just stood there silently. Kash had nothing to explain to Asia, but it was cute how she brought the kids to his game. He was honestly happy to see them, but if she thought this gesture would do to change anything about their relationship, she thought wrong. "You told me she was just your baby mama. What has changed? Why is that country bumpkin ass hoe here?"

"Asia, this is the reason I can't fuck with you. You out here acting a fucking fool in front of the world, in front of your kids. You worried about me and Heaven but not your fucking kids?" he asked.

"Fuck them kids!" She yelled. "I deleted the pictures off Instagram… I know I shouldn't had posted a picture of you with my kids. I'm sorry," she uttered, "Kash, you left me to be with her? That bitch doesn't have shit on me. Look at me."

"Yea, look at you." Agreeing, his eyebrows were dipped low in a scowl. With his hands smugly in front of him, clasped together and his shoulders squared, he stared at Asia.

"That bald head bitch. With that cheap ass dress and fake ass shoes she has on."

Kash laughed aloud and shook his head. "Asia, focus on your kids instead of what Heaven has on. Look at how you're acting in front of them."

"You don't care about how I'm acting in front of my kids. You get joy out of seeing me like this," she cried.

"Why would I get joy out of you crying?"

"I don't know, but you do. I told you I can't live without you."

"And I told you you can. I'm still here whenever you need me. I'm just no longer available the way you want me to be."

"But the kids miss you."

"G," he shook his head at her, "get your kids and go home. I miss them too, but that's not going to fix anything. You need to work on yourself, Asia." Kash called the kids' names. Heaven put Taiwan down, and all three began to walk towards Kash and Asia.

"Bye, kids!" Heaven yelled, waving at them.

"Bye!" They all sadly yelled back in unison.

"Girl, I'm glad you put her lil' dirty ass son down!" Esha said. "Lil' filthy ass kids. You probably got fleas on that pretty ass dress." Esha had her nose turned up as she walked over to Heaven.

"Esha, shut the fuck up." Lance wrapped his arm around her shoulder.

"Girl, fuck her. She saw I was here and sent her kids over here to see Kash, thinking that was gonna make me mad. But I always get the last laugh." She pursed her lips together.

"I know that's right, friend."

Heaven, Esha, and Lance began to walk over towards Kash. As they approached him, he stood there with his hands on his hips and his head hung, wondering how the hell he attracted this crazy ass woman.

"Aye, you good, G?" Lance asked, walking past Kash with his arm wrapped around Esha's shoulder.

The two stopped in mid stride on the side of Kash. Lance couldn't do anything but feel sorry for Kash, but like he had said, Kash and Heaven's business wasn't his.

Kash looked up, and the first face he saw was Heaven's. She was now standing in front of him. He smiled. "Yeah, I'm good." He wrapped his arm around her back, pulling her to him.

The men were handed a brick of twenties and two trophies. Kash, Heaven, Lance, and Esha stood together, and the men took pictures with their ladies. This was a tradition every summer in Kash's neighborhood. Before the end of the summer, the hood hosted a basketball game and block party which Kash and Lance planned to attend tomorrow.

***

The time on the dashboard displayed 10:30 p.m. as Heaven sat on the driver's side of Kash's Camaro. The windows were down, and they were doing eighty miles per hour on the I290 Expressway. Snapping her fingers to Come and Talk to Me by Jodeci, she licked her nude painted lips and smiled. Putting her foot to the brake, she reduced her speed, noticing the traffic beginning to slow down. Briefly looking over at Kash, she smiled at him. His seat was laid all the way back as he rubbed her thigh with one hand and smoked a raw cone full of exotic weed with the other. She was happy being with him. Although things were fairly new between them, she could honestly say he made her heart feel something, and pure happiness was an emotion she hadn't felt in a while. The smile she wore on her face wasn't forced or because she had to put on an act in front of her family. This smile was unadulterated.

"Get off right here," Kash said as they approached the Independence Avenue exit. "Make a left." He instructed when they reached the light. Afterwards, Kash turned the radio up another notch. He, along with Heaven, sang the lyrics to Joceci's song. In rhythm with one another, the two had their own little duet concert in the front seat of Kash's car.

There you are again with the same smile each day

I wanna know what it is to make me feel this way

I wish I could grab you, tell you what it means to me.

"What you know about this, youngin'?" Kash asked before taking another pull from his weed.

"This is that classic R&B shit. My age doesn't have anything to do with my love for good music. When I was going through my little teenage heartbreak, all I did was listen to music that made me cry. This song reminded me of you."

"Yeah?"

"Yeeeep! My daddy used to hate it. Even to this day, I will turn my television up to the max and vibe out on some good ole R&B music."

"Me too, baby." Kash agreed, his voice trailing off a bit. Sitting up in his seat and retrieving his gun from his hip, he took it off safety and sat it on his lap. They were in the heart of the hood where niggas blew their guns without warning, and he wanted to make sure Heaven was protected.

Heaven looked at Kash, trying to see what he was doing. When she saw the gun on his lap, she let out an exasperated breath. "You love that gun, don't you?"

"Yep. Park right here." They pulled in front of the bar. "This the hood, baby. It's better to be caught with it than without. I told you I keep it on me."

"Kash," Heaven said in disgust. It was not from the gun, especially since she had been around guns and hood men her entire life. Derrick had at least ten guns stashed around their house. Plus, her family made sure she was always protected growing up. Nevertheless, her disgusted tone came from her pulling up to a spot in the ghetto. Heaven had never been on a date in the hood, and this made her look at Kash a little differently. She knew she was worth more than a cheap ass dinner at a rundown bar.

Plus, the neighborhood didn't look safe. This was nothing like the neighborhoods Esha had taken her to.

This would be her third time visiting the gutters of Chicago, and she was not feeling this. Hell, she'd never been to the slums of her own town.

Heaven was a little bougie, she had to admit, and the sight of trash everywhere repulsed her. It was written all over her face. It wasn't on purpose, but as she sat there, her nose was turned up. Everything just looked so outdated and dirty, including the building Kash told her to park in front of. She prayed they weren't going inside. It looked like a hole in the wall. The building was white with one window and a tinted glass door.

"What's wrong?" he asked. Her face was screwed up terribly. He knew this wasn't her type of scene. She was still dressed in her dress and heels from earlier, and her jewelry alone looked like it was worth more than the entire block.

"Are we going in this building right here?" She pointed.

"Yeah, I want you to meet my cousin, Nadia," he said. "She owns the spot, her and my uncle."

"Oh, okay," she replied. "Dinner and wine would've been nice too."

"We can do all that bougie shit in your town, but while you're in Chicago, we gon' do Chicago shit. You know I wouldn't put you in any danger, right?"

"Yes, I know, Kashmir. That's why you keep it on you, right?"

Kash smirked. "Kashmir, huh? Niggas don't call me Killa for shit, baby. You're always gonna be good with me." He rubbed her thigh for reassurance before opening the passenger's door and climbing out. "Turn the car off." Closing the door, he walked around to the driver's side, opened Heaven's door, and helped her out. He held his gun in his hand, inside the front of his black jogging shorts, while he placed his other arm around her shoulders.

Heaven intertwined her fingers with his. Seconds later, they were walking inside Nadia's establishment and taking a seat at the bar.

"Yo!" Kash yelled over the music, grabbing Nadia's attention. She was standing on the other end, near the corner of the bar, leaned over, talking to a group of women. Still, it was pretty empty in the bar for a Friday. He watched as she excused herself. She picked up a bottle of Patron and shot glasses before making her way over to Kash and Heaven.

"Hey, cousin," she smiled, sitting the bottle down.

"Damn, G. You brought the Tron over here. What you tryna say, a nigga an alcoholic?"

"Kash, don't start. You're in a bar. What do most people go to a bar to do? You know what? Don't even answer that." She smiled.

"I didn't even come to drink tonight, shorty. I came here for the hot wings."

"Kash, stop it!" She laughed.

"Straight up, cuz. And I wanted to introduce you to my baby, Heaven."

"So, you're saying you brought this beautiful young lady all the way here, to the hood, just to meet your favorite cousin?" she asked, pursing her lips together.

"Yeah, and to get some wings," he replied.

"Yeah, yeah." Nadia sat a glass in front of Kash and in front of Heaven. She poured them both a shot. Before they got off to a bad start, Nadia decided to introduce herself. She knew who Heaven was, remembering her from the pictures Kash had shown her weeks ago. "How are you, Heaven?"

"I'm well." She had a slight grin on her face. She wasn't really sure how Nadia knew who she was. Heaven looked at Kash.

He scooted his stool closer to hers. "I told Nadia all about you and Baby K. That's how she knows your name."

"Baby K? I heard you call Kamelia that the other day. I like it. Killa K and Baby K. That's cute."

"Kash, I know you don't have this poor girl calling

you Killa K." Nadia laughed.

"Only when I got her bent over," he said jokingly, winking his eye, but he was serious.

Heaven's mouth dropped open widely as she hit his chest.

"Just nasty!" Nadia smirked.

"He is so disrespectful."

Tonight, things were a little slow and quiet, so Nadia had time to spend with her cousin and his baby, as he called her.

While the other bartender helped the rest of the patrons, Kash shared stories with Heaven and Nadia about his dreams of being in the NBA as a kid. He told them about how smart he was in school, but it was hard living a square life with all the invoking and tempting things he witnessed on a daily basis. His mother didn't want him to be shit, and it showed. She kept nothing but no good men around him, and she never supported his NBA dreams.

Although Lance hung around Kash, doing dumb shit, he worked and made his money the legit way. Kash loved Lance for that. He had to live vicariously through him, knowing that one day he would be stable enough to live just as legit. They had known each other since the 3rd grade, and they both had some of the same goals and aspirations growing up. Basketball, money, and women. Nevertheless, they lived two different lifestyles.

"Kash was bad as hell when he was a kid." Nadia cut in to share some embarrassing stories of her own.

"I can tell."

"Naw, boo. He has calmed down a lot. He even has a chilled demeanor now, but that hasn't always been the case."

"Whaaat?" Heaven said, all ears. She leaned into the bar with her elbows on top and her chin nestled on the back of her hands. She wanted to hear this.

"Heaven, girl, this nigga was so fucking mischievous. I loved him, because he was my cousin, but I hated his ass at the same time. He done put a dead mouse on my pillow before. I can remember one time when Auntie Doreen sent Kash to our house for two weeks because she was sick and couldn't take care of him. This nigga put some firecrackers in a pot, and while I was sleep, he snuck into my room and lit them. I thought I was dead when I heard what sounded like gunshots. After that, I started locking my bedroom door at night to keep his crazy ass out."

"Come on, man, don't start. You know I had ADHD when I was a shorty. I had a fucked-up childhood, bro." He chuckled.

"Yeah, and my father beat the ADHD right up out

yo' ass."

"Real talk!" Kash agreed, shaking his head and laughing. For the next ten minutes, they continued to share stories until Kash's phone began to vibrate in his pocket. He pulled it out and answered. Hearing a panicky but hyped-up voice on the other end of the phone, telling him his mother was just beat up by her boyfriend, made Kash jump up from his seat. He hung up the phone and drank his last shot. "Come on, baby. Nadia, we gotta go. I'ma kill this nigga."

"What happened?"

"Doreen's bitch ass boyfriend about to make me hurt him. I gotta go over there."

"Be careful, Kashmir. It was nice meeting you, Heaven."

Fifteen minutes later, they were pulling up. Although it was so late in the evening, the block Kash's mother lived on was still live. Music was blasting from cars, and women were walking around in next to nothing while the men gambled. Of course, the liquor and drugs were in abundance as everyone, who was anyone, overcrowded the sidewalks and streets.

Leaning over, Kash blew the horn with urgency. After getting that phone call about his mother and her bitch ass boyfriend, he was not in the mood to be fucked with. "Get the fuck out the street!" He yelled at a few people standing in the street directly in front of his mother's driveway.

"Nigga, what?" a male's voice said, turning around. He was brawny as hell and ready to get his ass whooped.

"Nigga, you heard me. Get yo' bitch ass out the street, nigga," Kash said.

The guy decided he would walk up to Kash's car to see who was trying to disrespect him, but he quickly changed his mind when Kash opened the door and stepped out slightly. Although he was still young, niggas looked up to him. He was one of the big homies to so many of the people who lived in the area. Niggas in his hood respected him. He fed the hood. He invested in the people he saw potential in, the same way Dre had done for him in his hood. Plus, everyone saw what happened to his mother a little while ago, so they knew he'd pulled up ready to dead anybody.

"Oh, shit, that's Killa. What's up, G?" another guy said, walking to the sidewalk.

"Oh shit. My bad, Killa," the other guy said, backing off. Niggas began dispersing, moving out the way and onto the sidewalk as well.

Kash got back inside the car and slammed the door. "Pull in right here." He pointed, directing Heaven to pull into his mother's driveway. He leaned forward and pulled his gun off his hip. He opened his door.

"Kash, what are you doing? Where are we?" Heaven asked, looking around nervously. Although this was the same neighborhood Esha had brought Heaven to before, they were on a different block, and it didn't look familiar to her, so she was afraid. This looked like the type of neighborhoods her father warned her about, and she was afraid. Why did he need a gun? They were only going inside his mother's house.

"Turn the car off," he instructed. "This my mama crib. You're good, baby," he promised, noticing how nervous she was. It was written all over her face as she looked around in all directions. "Come here," he said, pulling her face to his and pecking her lips. "You're safe with me."

"I think I want to get out the car."

"You think? Staying out here in the car wasn't an option anyway." He smirked before stepping out and slamming the door. His face had a grimace on it as he cocked his gun before walking to the driver's side. He opened Heaven's door, and she wasted no time jumping out. She was not about to stay out there by herself with all these crazy looking people.

"I got you!" Kash said. He kept his gun in his hand as he grabbed Heaven's shaky hand, using his thumb to rub the back of her hand to calm her shot nerves.

The guy who called Kash's phone to inform him

about what happened ran up to him and reiterated his story.

"Shit, we was all out here chilling. I was sitting on the porch, with your moms, drinking. I had just poured her a cup of D'usse when her boyfriend came home, tripping."

"Word?"

"I was sitting down on the steps when the nigga stormed past me and pulled her up off her seat. I was caught off guard because I didn't understand what the problem was. But when Jeff slapped the fuck outta her, I had to get involved," he explained. "I charged that nigga. I pushed Doreen out the way and hemmed him up. I grabbed my gun off my hip. I was about to pistol whip that nigga, but you know how Miss Doreen is over dude. She begged me not to hit him. She pulled me up off him, so I had no choice but to let shit be."

Kash shook his head. "Yeah, I know. G, thanks for looking out."

"No problem."

Heaven was silent but in shock. Although Kash was upset after the phone call he had gotten while they were at his cousin's bar, she didn't know his mother had just gotten beaten up. She didn't know his mother was in an abusive relationship. Honestly, she didn't know anything about her. Hell, Kash never talked about his mother to her.

"Come on, baby," Kash said, walking ahead of Heaven. They were still hand and hand as they ascended the stairs. Upon reaching the front door, Kash tucked Heaven behind him and put a key he'd taken from his pocket into the lock. Twisting the doorknob, they walked inside the home through the kitchen. It looked like a tornado had hit it. Furniture was turned over, and clothing was everywhere. It was clear that an altercation had broken out between the two.

"Kash," Heaven whispered.

"Be quiet." They stepped over an empty bottle of liquor. "You gotta excuse the crib." He was embarrassed, to say the least, as they walked into the living room to an even bigger mess. A ripped sofa, broken coffee table, and a foul odor made the house feel abandoned.

Heaven wasn't used to this. The look on her face was that of pure repugnance.

In the corner of the room, Doreen's boyfriend lay comfortably, stretched out on a Laz-E-Boy, fast asleep.

"Stay right here." Kash let go of Heaven's hand and walked over to Jeff. Without any words, Kash tapped the bottom of his foot with the nose of his pistol, wanting to wake him up before tearing into his ass.

"Man, what the fuck?" He opened his eyes and saw Kash standing there. "Doreen!" he yelled. "You done called yo' bitch ass son over here? Nigga, go get me a muthafucking beer and get the fuck out my face before I beat yo' ass worser than what I did to yo' hoe ass mama." Grinning, Jeff put his arms across his chest and crossed his legs at the ankles.

Without a word, Kash smirked and smashed the butt of his pistol against Jeff's face.

"Argh!" Jeff screamed from the impact. The sound of bones cracking was tumultuous as Kash commenced to pulverizing Jeff's face. Ear piercing screams and pleas filled the room as Jeff begged Doreen to save him from the wrath of Kash.

Kash was in a trance. Jeff's pleas meant absolutely nothing to him. He was tired of the control men had over Doreen. His scowl told it all. His calm aggression wouldn't allow him to speak words, but the way he bit down on his bottom lip while striking Jeff repeatedly made it known that his intentions were murderous. The only thing he saw was himself beating Jeff until he was deceased.

All Heaven could do was stand there, astonished. She didn't know how to stop Kash's attack. Kash was working Jeff, hitting him in his face over and over with his gun. His face was a bloody mess as were Kash's hands and shirt. Even a few of Jeff's teeth had flown from his mouth and onto the floor.

"Kash!" Heaven screamed, running up behind him,

afraid to touch him or intervene. She didn't know if Kash would mistakenly hit her. "Somebody help me." She'd never seen so much blood in her life. Kash wasn't a skinny man, but he wasn't a big nigga either. Still, he possessed strength she didn't know he had. At this point, Heaven didn't know what to do besides scream his name. Kash was always so laidback, so this was way out of character for him. He was truly in rare form. "Kashmir, baby, please stop," she cried, but Kash didn't hear her.

"You think you can keep putting your hands on my OG, and I'ma let that shit ride?" He grabbed a hold of Jeff's shirt, putting his gun back in his waistband. He punched Jeff in the nose. Blood sprayed from the bridge of his nose. The tears that had began to fall from Jeff's eyes mixed in with his deep red, burgundy color blood.

"I'm sorry, man," Jeff cried.

"Nigga, save your sorries for Doreen." He punched him again.

"Kash, please stop." Heaven begged again as his mother came running from the back with her hair all over her head.

She looked a mess. Her face looked like she had been in a cat fight. Random scratches were everywhere, as if Jeff purposely wanted to fuck her face up. She was just as light skinned as Kash, so the abuse she endured tonight and over the years was evident, especially the red and purple handprint.

"Kashmir Harris, stop this bullshit right now," Doreen yelled, running up behind him and grabbing the hand he was hitting Jeff with. "Get the hell off my man. You're always getting in the middle of my relationships. I fucking hate you!" she yelled.

Kash heard her and yanked his arm from her grasp. He pushed her back, making her stumble backwards. She fell to the floor, and Kash backed away from Jeff. The room fell silent as he smirked. Here he was, ready to murder Jeff because of what he had done to her, and here she was, telling him she hated him. He couldn't believe his ears, but this didn't surprise him.

"That's crazy, Ma."

Doreen stood from the floor and pushed Kash out the way. Running over to be by Jeff's side, she held his face. "Baby, let me see." She got on her knees to examine Jeff's injuries. "All this fucking blood."

"You hate me, Ma?" Kash asked, but she ignored him. "Doreen, you hate me?"

"Yes, Kashmir. I fucking hate your ass. You're the reason I can't keep a stable relationship."

"All I ever try to do is protect you from these niggas who beat your ass and use you for what they think you have."

Heaven walked over and grabbed his arm, pulling at him, but he was stuck in place. Kash couldn't believe the truth was finally coming out, and after today, he swore he was washing his hands of her. "You ain't never been a mother to me, but I still pay the mortgage on this rundown ass house for you to sit and move this faggot ass nigga in here to beat on you. Look at your fucking face." He yanked away from Heaven and walked over to his mother. Grabbing her arm, he forced her to stand up and face him. "Look at your fucking face, Doreen."

"Kashmir, let me the fuck go. He didn't mean to hit me so hard. It was my fault. He told me about letting these young niggas on the porch, and I didn't listen."

"Man, what the fuck is you talking about? You got scratches and shit all over your damn face, G. This nigga been beating yo' ass at least once a week." Kash frowned with tears in his eyes. He moved his mother out the way and reached for Jeff's throat. Flinching, Doreen stepped in between them and pushed Kash. She slapped his face while yelling.

"You need to learn how to mind your own business, Kashmir. Stay in a child's place."

"Me minding my own business means me cutting you the fuck off indefinitely. I'm your fucking child, Doreen. You gotta son that'll murder whoever, and you sitting here, letting this nigga kick yo' ass. You pathetic as fuck, man. Just know that when this nigga kill you, I'ma collect a big ass check."

"Get the hell out my house right now. You and this thing you done brought up in here."

Heaven grabbed his arm again. "Let's just leave, Kash."

"Are you serious, Ma?" he asked, clearly hurt. Squinting his eyes as tears finally fell from them, his face instantly turned red as he took a deep breath.

"Come on, Kash." Heaven stepped in front of him and grabbed his arms. Looking up at him, she began to tear up as well. She felt bad for him. She had no idea that Kash's mother was this way. No wonder he never talked about her. She could only imagine Kash's childhood.

"Yes, get the fuck out my house, Kashmir," Doreen shouted, and Kash reached into his pocket. He pulled a stack of money out and threw it on the floor.

"Heaven, meet my mother, Doreen," he said, still looking at his mother with tears blinding his vision. Blinking, he wiped them away. "Doreen, this is my daughter's, your granddaughter's, mother, Heaven. I have a five-year-old daughter who you will never meet," he said. "You hate me, Ma? You'll give me up, your only child, to be with this nigga?" He frowned as Heaven kept her hand to his chest, empathizing with him. His muscles flexed as he spoke with malice. His voice was no longer laidback. He was screaming, unable to control his emotions. Kash couldn't believe his mother finally spoke her truth. "I'm done with you, Doreen. That's $10,000. As long as you keep dealing with these types of niggas, you can stay the fuck outta my life."

NINE

Kash never really brought women around his mother. Admittedly, he was embarrassed of her. She was an alcoholic who didn't give a fuck about him. At times, his heart possessed the same hate for Doreen that she had for him because he never felt like he was a priority of hers. Still, she was his mother, and it was his obligation to respect her, even if she didn't respect him. He had to. She gave him life, and for that reason alone, she deserved his upmost respect.

With Doreen being the type of woman she was when it came to men, when it comes time for Kamelia to start dating, Kash was going to make sure she knew what types of men she should date. He was going to make sure she was able to see the difference between a good man and a knucklehead from a mile away. Kash was going to mold Kamelia into a respectable woman, a great woman that any good man would love to be with, while a broke, abusive nigga would know he didn't stand a chance. He wasn't going to have it any other way.

As a kid, he went through hell with his mother falling for men who used her as a punching bag and her home as a drug spot. The saying, you are who you attract, had to be true. It was as if she had the words beat me written across her forehead because every single man she dealt with beat her senseless. Although she never beat Kash physically, it was the way she mentally and emotionally tore him down, inflicting her own hurt and insecurities onto him.

It was a wonder Kash didn't grow up doing the same things to women, beating their asses just for existing. However, he did grow up not really knowing how to love and being afraid to love, scared that the woman he gave his heart to would eventually hurt him in some type of way because that was what his mother, the first woman he ever loved, had done to him time and time again. She never had time for him because she was too busy putting herself first, and he prayed Heaven was different. Doreen had really fucked Kash up. He just prayed the life Heaven's father provided her afforded her quality time with their daughter, Kamelia. Kash needed that assurance. He was traumatized at an early age, and that was the reason he couldn't stomach being around Asia when she mistreated her kids.

An hour after leaving his mother's home, Kash and Heaven were pulling up in front of his five-bedroom, brick house on the north side of Chicago. With gated fences and a manicured lawn, the outside of Kash's dwelling mirrored everyone else's on his block. Choosing to move far away from his old neighborhood put him in a position to live comfortably. Everyone knew where he was from, but no one knew where he lived. Kash was smart. He always thought beyond the projects, and he knew he had to be both book and street smart in order to succeed in life. He invested in himself, and he wasn't willing to lose anything he had for anyone. Not even Doreen.

Heaven would be the first and only woman he invited into his home. But Heaven was different. She was used to having things, and her mentally was somewhat like his. She wasn't willing to lose in life for anyone. She was the mother of his child, and she'd just witnessed a very touchy part of his life - his mother and all her toxicity. She got to witness Doreen's fucked up ways up close and personal. When it came to his relationship with his mother, he became this vulnerable child, and he despised it. Heaven saw his tears and how his mother played with his emotions. This was normal for him. He was used to being talked to like he wasn't shit by the one person he should've meant everything to.

Aside from the forest preserve, his home was the one place he found peace. When he was home, nothing else in the world mattered. His energy was positive, and he refused to allow negative vibrancies in.

Kash couldn't be alone tonight. He was too caught

up in his feelings. He wouldn't be able to sleep. He needed Heaven by his side, and he didn't want to spend the night at her apartment. He wanted to be in the comforts of his own home and bed, in his own serene space where the walls didn't talk nor tell his secrets, where he felt free to solemnly feel whatever it was his heart needed to feel.

As soon as they walked into his home, Kash told Heaven to make herself comfortable. She followed him down the long hallway, stopping in front of a humongous bedroom. Heaven pulled the back of his shirt. He stopped walking and turned around to look at her.

She grabbed the front of his shirt, pulling him to her before wrapping her arms around him. Of course, he hugged her back.

Remanence of his emotions settled within the corners of his eyes as he bear hugged her. The feeling of affection made him feel good, especially after hearing his mother tell him she hated him. His heart needed Heaven and all her love, but first, he needed to get away for at least ten minutes. So, he unwrapped from their embrace.

"I'ma go run a shower. The bedroom is right there." He pointed Heaven to the room while he made his way to the master bathroom that was next door to his bedroom. He closed the door and walked over to the shower. He turned it on before flipping the lid to the toilet close and taking a seat. Sighing, he was now in deep thought and ready for the night to end. He rested his elbows into his legs and leaned his head down. He stayed in that position until the bathroom began to fill with fog. Still, his mind was in overdrive as he stood up and began to strip from his clothes. He entered the shower. In front of the water, he just stood there with his eyes closed, letting the water massage his face and body. Feeling a presence enter behind him and a set of hands touch his back, he knew Heaven was there, especially when he felt her breasts and lips brush up against his back.

Silently, they stood there together. This was the second time that day they'd showered together. The only difference with this shower was that sex was the furthest thing from their minds. Instead, Heaven hugged Kash from behind, holding him. The water pouring down on them both, possibly ruining Heaven's hair, but she didn't care. She needed to reassure Kash that he was loved. Yes, she despised the way he had done her in the past, but she could never bring herself to hate him. The man he is, was way different from the way he was raised.

"Kashmir," she kissed his back, "I'm sorry you had to go through that."

"It's all good." He wiped water from his face. "She keep showing me who she really is, and I keep letting her back in my life."

"That's your mother, Kash, so you constantly letting her back in your life is understandable. You want her to be someone she will never be."

"I've done everything for her." Kash turned to look at Heaven. "I got other shit to deal with. That shit she was talking about don't faze me. All the things she has put me through since a shorty, I'm built for it." He looked down as she looked up at him. "Look at you." He smiled, moving her wet hair from her face. "Your hair all wet and shit. This mafuckin' wig bet not slip off in your sleep. I'm not tryna wake up to you in no jailhouse braids." He smirked, pushing her hair to her back.

She cocked her head to the side and wrapped her arms around him. "That was cute." She smiled. "But Kash, it's okay to be hurt right now. You don't have to do or say anything to make me laugh. I've been through some shit with my mother too, so I know how you feel." She squinted. "Anika has always hurt me, and I take her back every time too. It's like a toxic ass love that you can't help but to feel. You just want that person to love you as much as you love them, and they break your heart every time, piece by piece. I know the feeling, Kashmir. Trust me."

Kash cleared his throat. Everything Heaven was saying was how he felt, but of course, he wasn't ready to really talk about it. "Man, that's lil' shit." He sucked his teeth. "I'm used to it."

"Well, you shouldn't be. I'm no one to judge. Me and my mama be on the verge of fighting. I be ready to bash her fucking face in, but something always tells me not to. My daddy told me that I only get one mother, but I just want you to know that no matter what we been through in the past and what we might go through in the future, I love you. I always have, and I always will."

"That's good to know. I love you too."

"Baby K loves you as well. Although she hasn't met you yet."

Kash hugged Heaven tightly. "My heart is missing something, and I think it's Kamelia." Honestly, nothing could contain the pain he felt when it came to his mother but having Heaven here with him made Kash feel better.

Ten minutes later, Kash was taking a seat on his bed with his towel wrapped around his waist. He leaned back, intertwining his fingers and cuffing them behind his head. Staring up at the ceiling, deep in thought, he heard Heaven enter the bedroom with two shot glasses and a bottle of Patron in her hands. He couldn't believe his mother had once again chosen a man over him. Still, he loved her. He would give his mother the world if only she loved him the same.

"Here," Heaven said. She was dressed in one of Kash's big t-shirts that swallowed her body. Handing

Kash a shot she'd just poured seconds ago, she climbed into bed and sat on the side of him, Indian style. She stared at him, smiling, happy to be in his presence. Doreen had her fucked up, talking about she hated Kash. Now, she would love him and overcompensate for her love, just so he knew Doreen's opinion was invalid.

TEN

Heaven had been awake for two hours now, getting herself acquainted with Kash's house. She walked through all five bedrooms, which were furnished with a bed, TV stand, a television, and dressers. It took everything in Heaven not to climb into every bed and smell the sheets. There had to be the scent of a woman somewhere. His home had a woman's feel to it, so she knew she wasn't the only woman who had been in his home. She had a feeling Asia and her kids had been there as well. Why else would he need so many bedrooms? As she walked through all four bathrooms, she looked through the medicine cabinets and underneath the sinks. Still, she came up empty.

She looked through the living room, dining room, kitchen, and basement. Kash was a neat freak. Every morsel of his home was spotless. It was clear he had expensive taste as well. Everything his childhood home didn't have, he made sure to purchase it when he was able to afford it himself. His Azure LHR sofa, that cost at least $12,000, told the story of the type of money Kash had. Heaven giggled, not knowing how he would keep his cream-colored furniture and walls clean when Kamelia came over or how he would keep her little handprints off his glass tables and stainless-steel appliances.

After searching his home and coming up empty, she went back into the bathroom and looked at her reflection in the mirror.

"I'm trippin'." She licked her lips and closed her eyes. "After all the shit he went through last night, you're really in here searching this man's home?" she asked herself. With Kash's oversized t-shirt on, she looked down at herself. His shirt was so big that it touched her knees. Standing on the sides of her feet, she shook her head. "Heaven, he gave you the clothes off his back to sleep in." She sucked her teeth. "He cried in front of you." Looking back up at the mirror, she moved in a little closer, remembering her hair had gotten wet the night before. After a little inspection, she realized her lace was okay. She ran her fingers through her hair. It was still soft and manageable; only now, it had a cute natural wave to it.

Feeling her phone vibrate, she lifted her cell phone and looked at it as a FaceTime call came through from Derrick. She quickly silenced it. She still hadn't figured out how she was going to tell Kash she was engaged. Walking back to Kash's bedroom on her toes, she crept back into bed and climbed on top of him.

"Kash." Bending over, Heaven whispered into Kash's ear. Afterwards, she began softly kissing him all over his face. He stirred a little, but he did not open his eyes. "Kashmir Harris," she sang into his ear. "Wake up, sir." Sitting up and straddling him, she just stared at him. He looked exactly like their daughter, even while he was asleep.

The more she looked at Kash, she knew she would choose him over Derrick any day. Heaven came from wealth while Derrick was trying to come up off her family. Although Kash didn't grow up with a silver spoon in his mouth, it was obvious he had his own money. In her heart, she felt they were meant to be, especially since she let him go a long time ago, but somehow, here they were, here together.

"Get yo' heavy ass off me," Kash said with his eyes still closed.

"I am not heavy." She frowned. Leaning back down, she laid her head on his shoulder. "How are you feeling today, Kash?" She kissed his cheek.

"I'm coolin', shorty." He raised his arms and stretched. "How you feeling, baby?" Turning his head to the side, he kissed her shoulder.

"I'm great," she said into the side of his face.

"Did you sleep good?"

"Yes. Now, I'm up and ready to start my day. Let's

go get some breakfast."

"What if I cook breakfast for you instead?"

She sat up with her face frowned. "Can you even cook? No offense, baby daddy, but I would rather go out." She laughed, squeezing his chin in between her fingers.

"No offense but don't call me baby daddy. That shit is disrespectful. And yes, I know how to cook. I know you're used to chefs cooking for you and shit. I can give you that too, but I'm personally offering you my services."

"First of all, Kashmir, I cook for myself. I don't have chefs and butlers, okay!" Heaven muffed Kash as she climbed off him.

"Yeah, whatever. But fuck it, I'll take yo' hungry ass somewhere to eat. Fat ass."

Kash sat up and took the covers off. He stood up, exposing his body. He was completely naked as he cupped his erection with his left hand and reached under his pillow for his phone with the right.

Scrolling through his missed calls and text messages, he frowned, disturbed by the amount of missed calls and messages he had from Asia.

"What's wrong?" Heaven asked, standing up in the bed and walking over to him. She wrapped her arms around his neck and hugged him.

"Nothing." Kash laid his phone down on the bed and hugged her around her waist. He couldn't tell her what was bothering him. Heaven pursed her lips and looked him in his eyes.

"Are you sure?" She squinted.

"Yeah, I'm sure."

"Well, let me see," she said softly with one eyebrow raised. "Unlock your phone."

Kash smirked. "Hell naw, man." He removed Heaven's arms from around his shoulders. "It ain't shit for you to see in my phone."

"What the fuck you mean it ain't shit in your phone for me to see?" She tapped his forehead with her hand.

"G, watch your hand," he said, grabbing her wrist. "I'm not with that hitting shit, shorty."

"Well, let me see your damn phone."

"Man, Heaven, it's too early for this shit." He shook his head, turning to walk away. Heaven was pissing him off. It seemed like they had an argument about something stupid every time they were around each other.

Kash tried to prevent an unwanted argument by walking away. Heaven wouldn't be Heaven if she didn't confront the situation. She climbed from the bed and followed him.

"I just wanted to see what the hell got you so bothered. Let's not start things off holding secrets."

He turned back around to look at her. "I don't have any secrets, baby. But if you're gonna try to make me feel guilty, make sure you're not holding any secrets from me." Walking back over to the bed, he picked up his phone and unlocked it. Scrolling through his call log, he showed her everything.

"This girl is crazy, Jo," he said.

"Why did she call you so many times? She does know it is over between y'all, right?" Heaven cocked her head to the side.

"Yeah, she know."

"So, you need to call her and tell her to leave you the fuck alone."

"I'm not thinking about her. I don't have shit to tell her."

"Why not?"

"I don't like drama, Heaven. I don't like to be questioned either. If you can't take my word as law and trust me, we don't need to be together. We can just co-parent and be cordial. I showed you my phone. What more do you want?"

"We can just co-parent? Kash, kiss my ass. We not co-parenting shit, and you not going nowhere. I trust you. I just don't trust her."

"Okay, if you trust me then drop it. Fuck her."

Kash and Heaven got dressed. Afterwards, he took her to a popular breakfast spot in Chicago. Out on the balcony, they enjoyed the sun and warm air. With a glass of Champagne, Heaven tried her best not to stare at Kash, but she couldn't help it. She was mesmerized by him as she watched him while he laughed at something in his phone. His honey brown skin, brown eyes, and beautiful smile had her in a daze. This here was a long time coming. She lifted her glass of Champagne up to her lips and took a sip. Sitting her glass down, her eyes fell on her left hand and onto her ring finger. Noticing the tan around the area where her ring used to sit, she moved her hand from the table, put it on her lap, and took a deep breath.

"What's wrong?" Kash asked, looking up from his phone.

"Nothing, babe." She looked at him as she took another sip from her glass.

"Are you sure?"

"No, I'm not sure," she said honestly.

"Okay." He sat his phone down. "Talk to me."

"Kash, I…" She smacked her lips and smiled. "Nothing." She shook her head.

"Didn't you say some shit about us not keeping secrets?" He looked at her. Scooting closer to the table, he leaned in. "Talk to me."

"It's just that I live a whole different life in Atlanta."

"I'm sure you do."

"I want you to come home with me, but I don't want anything about my life to come out while we are there. I would rather tell you before."

"Okay, I'm listening," he said, scratching his head.

She looked down at the table before looking back up at him.

"What's up?"

"My life is crazy with Kamelia and my…" She swallowed hard.

"Your what?"

"Kash, I'm engaged," she said, putting her hand back on the table.

Kash smirked as he squinted his eyes and looked at her hand. "Okay, so call the nigga and tell him the engagement is off."

"Are you serious?" she asked, frowning.

"Dead ass serious," he replied as the waitress came over with their food. "I don't want to talk about it no more." He moved back slightly as their food was laid out on the table. They both were silent until the waitress walked away.

"Kash, I don't know who you think I am, but you don't get to say what you have to say and then shut the fucking conversation down. I'm not Asia. I'm gon' say what the hell I need to say." She cocked her head to the side. He was silent. "Now, I gave you the opportunity to break things off with Asia without even pressuring you. I even gave you time to make sure with me is where you wanted to be. You owe me the same thing, Kashmir."

"I don't owe you shit, and I don't give a fuck about your engagement." His facial expression never changed. It stayed normal as he talked while cutting into his steak. "But I tell you what you are going to do; you're gonna break that engagement off with dude, and I'm gonna be there when you do it. I know you don't give a fuck about him, or you wouldn't even be here with me. I'm the nigga you love and will never get over. Believe, I'm not going nowhere, and neither are you. You and that nigga is through. Do you hear me?"

"Yes, Kashmir. I hear you." She smiled, slightly turned on by his assertiveness.

"Aight!" His facial expression was serious. "Get yo' ass up and give me a kiss," he said, and Heaven did as she was told. Leaning over the table, she pulled his face to hers and kissed him.

This conversation went better than she thought it would. Now that her little secret was out, she was able to breathe, but she didn't plan to take Kash with her when she broke it off with Derrick. She didn't want any conflict. She wanted to walk away from that relationship without any drama.

Heaven sat back in her seat, and together, she and Kash enjoyed breakfast. She dug into her strawberry cheesecake stuffed French toast, fried eggs, and bacon while Kash ate a steak, grits, scrambled eggs, and potatoes. They sat across from each other silently, both in deep thought.

Kash already knew about Heaven's engagement. He'd known it before she came to Chicago. That information was not a secret. Lance had already put him up on game, plus he saw the big ass ring on her finger when he was in her apartment that night. He was just waiting for her to mention it.

"Are you gonna eat that?" Heaven asked, breaking the silence. She picked up Kash's last piece of steak without giving him a chance to respond and stuffed it in her mouth.

"Really, G? I was finna eat that. You bogus as hell," he said, sucking his teeth.

"If you want it, Killa, come get it. You can have it

back." With a mouth full of steak, she stuck her tongue out, showing the chewed-up meat. She smiled.

Kash rubbed his beard and licked his lips. Leaning over the table, Heaven met him halfway and stuck her steak covered tongue into his mouth. He took it all in and pecked her lips before chewing.

"Kash, you are so disgusting." She laughed. "I can't believe you just ate that out my mouth."

"I done put my lips and tongue all in yo' pussy before, baby. I'll let you feed me anything, shorty."

Speechless, Heaven's mouth was wide open. "You are so fucking nasty."

"Hell yeah." He agreed. Licking his lips, he grinned. With his legs open and his elbow on the back of his seat, he watched Heaven through lustful eyes, watching as she shied away and looked down into her plate. She picked up her fork and played with the eggs that were left on her plate.

"I'm full," she said. She pushed her hair to the back and picked up her glass. She looked down into it, trying her best not to look at Kash.

"Aye!" Kash yelled, getting a waitress's attention.

"Must you be so ghetto? That's not even our waitress, Kash," she said, and he shrugged.

When the woman approached them, he asked for

the check. Afterwards, he sat silently.

Buzz, buzz! Heaven's phone began to vibrate. Seeing her father's name on her phone as a FaceTime call, she looked up at Kash.

"Answer that shit. That bet not be that goofy ass nigga. As a matter of fact, let me see your phone."

"Kash," Heaven said, sucking her teeth.

"Let me see," he demanded.

Heaven rolled her eyes and turned her phone around, allowing Kash to see her father's name on the screen.

"May I answer the phone now, Daddy?" she asked playfully as she quickly answered before Sno hung up.

"Mama!" Kamelia said excitedly. Heaven beamed, seeing her baby's face and hearing her voice.

"Hey, my love. What are you doing?"

"Nothing." She smacked her small lips. "Sitting here with Regan, playing with dolls. Look!" Kamelia showed Heaven the brand-new Barbie doll Reign had bought her.

"Ooouuu, Kamelia! She is pretty."

"I know. My papa said she is beautiful, just like me."

"Yes, Papa is right. You are very beautiful."

"Sister, look at mine." Excitedly, Regan put her doll in the camera.

"Yours is pretty too, Regan." Smiling, Heaven looked at Kash, who was looking directly at her. She knew he wanted to talk to Kamelia, or at least look at her, but she wanted them to engage with one another for the first time in person. "Guess what, Kamelia?"

"What?" she said shortly, distracted by Regan.

"I'm coming home next week, and I have someone for you to meet."

"Who do you want me to meet? I hope it's not one of your little friends because I don't need any new people in my life, Mama."

"Girl, shush!" Heaven laughed, shaking her head. She looked at Kash as he laughed out loud.

"Ma, who is that laughing? Is that your little friend?"

"No, Kamelia. I don't have any little friends."

"Big friend… Fuck you talking about?" Kash whispered.

"Where did you get that from? My little friend. Girl, you are something else."

"That's what Delilah said. Grandma Anika said you was in Chicago with your little friend."

"Kamelia, put your papa on the phone. I will talk to your little grown self later. I love you." Heaven blew a kiss at Kamelia before she passed the phone to Sno. After talking to Sno for about ten minutes, their check finally came, and afterwards, they left.

Kash pulled up in front of Heaven's building and parked. Leaning over, he puckered his lips, and Heaven kissed him.

"Be ready at six," he said.

"You love bossing me around, Kash." She leaned back and rolled her eyes. "What if I have something to do at six?"

"Cancel it and be ready at six. Wear some sexy shit like this too but put on some comfortable shoes." He pulled at her dress.

"I'll think about it." She rolled her neck and smiled as Kash pulled her by the back of her neck. He pulled her face to his and softly bit down on the side of her cheek.

"Ouch, Kash. Stop!" she whined. As she said that, they heard a soft tap at the window.

"Who the fuck is that?" He sat up and looked out the passenger's window. Heaven sucked her teeth, seeing the security officer from weeks ago standing there. She knew that if she didn't just agree with Kash and let him leave, there would for sure be a problem.

"Okay, I'll be ready at six." She took a deep breath and went to open the door. As she opened it, Kash also let down his passenger side window.

"G, don't knock on my muthafuckin' window. Fuck is wrong with you?"

"There is no parking here." He pointed to the sign as he had done with Esha.

"Kash, just leave." Heaven shook her head, closing the door. She felt an argument brewing. She saw things going left real fast.

"I know how to read, nigga. Take yo' bitch ass back in the building, and make sure my girl get in her crib safely before I pop yo' ass."

"Is that a threat?" he asked, pressing a button on the side of his radio.

"Nah, it's a promise, lil' nigga."

"Kash, I'm fine. Just leave. I don't need him to make sure I'm safe." The security officer walked away as Heaven looked at Kash pleadingly. "I'll call you when I'm ready."

"Aight, baby." He sat there until she walked inside the building before pulling off.

ELEVEN

Pulling up to the liquor store, Kash looked over at Heaven. It was still a little early in the day, about 7:45 in the evening, so the sun was starting to settle. She was beautiful as the setting sun's rays made her skin look radiant. Kash couldn't help himself. He cupped her chin with his hand, leaned over, and kissed her. Just like any liquor store, there were a few people hanging out in front. So, he made sure everybody knew she belonged to him. Through his slightly tinted windows, he kissed her slowly, sucking her lips as if they were a piece of candy.

Heaven inhaled Kash in, breathing in the smell of his minty breath and BVLGARI cologne. She tried her best to contain herself and not moan because they were in the mix of company.

"Daaaaammmmnn! It's like that, for real?" Esha asked, laughing, breaking up Kash and Heaven's make out session.

"Man, look at how you got this nigga, Heaven. I don't even know if I should still call you Killa, or just Kashmir, because you definitely on some soft shit tonight. We on our way to the hood, and this nigga in here tongue kissing and shit."

"Nigga, you know my mafuckin' name," Kash said, smirking, still looking at Heaven.

"Shit, no the fuck I don't. No offense, Heaven, but I ain't never seen my mans like this."

"Yeah, aight. When I pull this mafucka out and start spraying niggas…"

"Kash, stop with all that talk of shooting people. I don't want to hear that," Heaven said, and he shut the fuck up.

"Damn, she got you trained, my nigga." Lance mused.

"That's my girl." Esha laughed, grabbing Heaven's headrest. "Check that nigga how I be checking this nigga."

"Goofy ass." Pulling Esha to him by her shirt, Lance began to whisper in her ear.

"Man," Kash said, sucking his teeth.

"So, you don't be tongue kissing Esha?" Heaven asked.

"Hell yeah, I do. But that's normal behavior for me. I be kissing these big ass lips until these bitches get swollen," Lance said, licking Esha's lips.

"Lance, stop! Nasty."

"Clown ass," Kash said to Lance. "Did you want anything out the store?" he asked Heaven.

"No, I'm drinking whatever you are."

"Aight, I'll be right back." Today, he was in his all-black, Model X Tesla, ready to chill with the people who loved him. Opening the door and stepping from the car, he dusted off his faded wash, grey, ribbed, moto Balmain jeans. His entire outfit was the Balmain brand, including his black and gray crew neck shirt and black shoes. He had three platinum chains layered around his neck - twenty, twenty-four, and twenty-seven inches. All three were Jesus pieces. Around his wrist was a 42mm Ronde Solo Cartier watch. If dressed to impress was a person, his name would be Kashmir Harris.

Lance didn't sidestep either. Both men looked as if they modeled for the brands they were rocking. Lance wore a Burberry polo shirt and Burberry blue jean shorts. His shoes were Burberry as well, and around his neck he wore a gold Cuban chain link.

Kash left the car running while they left Heaven and Esha alone, and Esha immediately got out and walked to the driver's side. She got in and closed the door. Turning to look at Heaven, she smiled excitedly.

"So, you and Kash are a thing now?" Heaven didn't say anything. She just smiled. "I knew y'all would fall in love, friend. I am so happy for you. Now, you have to move to Chicago. But wait…" She grabbed Heaven's arm. "What about you and Derrick?"

"I'm leaving Derrick," she simply said. "Kash and I are going to Atlanta next week. He's gonna meet Kamelia, and we are going to go from there."

"Wooow, Heaven, that is so beautiful. This is almost like a fairytale story. The beautiful princess and the charming prince. You found love in a man who was forbidden to you, at least he should've been forbidden considering your age differences. But in the end, love wins. Kash is a great guy, Heaven, and I know Kamelia is going to love him. They look just alike."

"Yeah, he is great. Just from being around him and talking to him every day these past weeks, I've learned a lot about him."

"Like what?"

"Like his past didn't hinder his growth in life at all. And with the right woman, that woman being me," Heaven pointed to herself, "he will grow beyond expectations."

"Yes, bitch! You did not come here to play. We build our niggas up around here, baby. You got your man, and Kamelia got her father. I know that shit is right." Heaven and Esha high fived each other. "How did you tell Kash about Derrick?"

"I just came out and told him."

"How did you say it though?"

"Verbatim?"

"Yes, bitch, verbatim. And how did he react?"

"Well, we were at breakfast this morning, and I felt like I couldn't hide it anymore, especially after we had this big ass argument about him hiding his phone from me," she explained. "I don't remember everything I said, but long story short, I said 'Kash, I'm engaged'."

"And he said?"

"He told me to break it off. All I could do was say 'okay'."

"Yooo! Damn, friend, he must've really laid some great dick down on you."

"I mean, he's working with a lot, but bitch, I am so in love with Kash. I guess the love never left. I find myself just staring at him sometimes."

"So, y'all are together?"

"Yeah."

"Have you been to his house? Have you met Doreen yet?"

"Yes and yes."

"Bitch, this is definitely a serious relationship because he don't take nobody to his house, and he never takes women around his family."

"I guess." Heaven sighed, remembering the circumstances of how she met Kash's mother. "I'm thinking about keeping my apartment here in Chicago so that I can travel back and forth. That way I will still have my own space."

"I love it! For real, lil' sis, I am so happy for you and Kash. Y'all deserve each other."

"Thank you, Esha."

Kash and Lance's voices and chuckles ceased their conversation. Opening the door to get out, Kash stopped her and asked her to drive since she was already sitting in front.

She agreed, and minutes later, they were pulling up and parking in a lot on 13th Street. There was barely any room to maneuver around. The streets were packed with everyone in the neighborhood from teenagers to little boys and girls. The west side of Chicago did not discriminate. People who hadn't stepped foot in the neighborhood for months were out and about, dressed in their best clothing. Grown men and women stood around with their groups of friends, conversing, drinking liquor, partying, and getting reacquainted with past familiar faces. Elderly men and elderly women sat around in their yards, doing the same, chilling on their lawn chairs and talking shit while watching the young folks enjoy themselves. Even women with strollers, that held newborn babies inside, were outside, getting a taste of the hood's culture. Liquor was flowing, food was grilling, and the neighborhood was, without a doubt, full of positive energy.

Traditionally, they did this every year before school started back in September. There were basketball games, talent shows, school supply giveaways, and uniform and gym shoe drives, in which Kash donated thousands of dollars to the disadvantaged kids.

Opening Heaven's door, Kash helped her out the car. He held her hand as she switched past and stood on the side of him. Licking his lips, he threw his arm around her shoulders, and they stood there, waiting for Lance and Esha.

Lance and Esha walked around to the passenger side of the car, hand and hand. Handing Kash his car key, Esha offered to pour Heaven a cup of liquor. After they were all situated, Kash put his arm back around Heaven's shoulder while Esha and Lance held hands and began walking towards the big, open field where majority of the crowd stood around. As they made their way, Heaven smiled, holding Kash around his waist while he greeted and introduced her to the people he grew up with. He was like a hood celebrity. Everyone knew who he was, and they all loved him. The men he introduced Heaven to were cool. They dapped him and Lance up with no problems. They even cracked a few jokes with Heaven and Esha while the majority of the women sucked their teeth and turned their noses up.

She clearly wasn't from around there, and Esha was barely a familiar face, seeing as though her parents moved her to Park Ridge at an early age. Still, they knew who she was, specifically because she came to the hood often. But the women from out west were possessive over the men they grew up with, especially the men who were about something, and Kash had everything women like them desired - money, good looks, and power. He had everything to an outsider looking in. Kash's life was extravagant. He should've been willing to share everything with a girl who lived through the struggle of poverty with him, someone he could've bossed up while she helped boss him up. Yet, he chose to go out and get with a bitch who looked like she never struggled a day in her life. It was just like a nigga to come up and leave all the hood bitches behind.

"Aye, Lance, Kashmir," a male voice yelled out, causing the four to stop and look. A young man, who looked to be Kash's and Lance's age, who was dressed in a three-piece suit with the hat and dress shoes to match, began walking their way.

"Man, who the fuck is that, calling my real name and shit?" Kash asked, squinting. He couldn't make out the face, but he yelled back a quick "What's up?" He wasn't trying to be rude, plus he was watching his surroundings.

"That's Pastor Rocky," Esha said, laughing. His whole persona was a joke to her. "He look dumb as fuck."

"Aye, man, you can't be saying shit like that about a pastor. That nigga is anointed. Yo' ass going to hell, G," Kash said, chuckling.

"Why y'all call him pastor? He looks like a pimp."

"Because that nigga is a real pastor." They watched as Rocky began to walk their way.

Rocky was someone Kash and Lance used to hang with back in the day. All three men were from the projects. They were all tight, like brothers, until their teenage years.

They all took separate routes in life after entering high school. Kash began hanging out with Dre, Lance kept his head in the books, and Rocky became a father at sixteen and tried to live the life of a drug dealer. After getting caught serving on the block at the age of eighteen, he served three years in prison. By the time he came back home from prison, he was twenty-one and knew he needed to do something with his life in order to remain a free man. Jail made him want to do better in order to be there for his baby. Getting on a straight and narrow and finding God, he began studying the Christian religion. Soon enough, he threw himself deep into the church, working his way through the system and becoming an understudy. Now, he was a ghetto pastor, and his very own church, Holy Cross of Christ Missionary, was in the heart of the hood.

"Yo, what's good?" Lance said, raising his hand and smirking. "Aye, I'ma run to Ma Dukes's crib real quick. I don't wanna hear shit this nigga about to come over here preaching. G a whole pastor but out here kicking it like tomorrow ain't Sunday." Lance pimped off.

"I'm right behind you, baby." Laughing as she caught up with Lance, Esha left Kash and Heaven standing there.

"Fuck." Kash shook his head. This wasn't the time or place to hear the word. He was out here trying to kick it. Kash had a cup of liquor in his hand and a gun on his hip. "G, do you go to church?" He took a long drink from his cup.

"No. I've never been. Why?" Heaven whispered back.

"Yo, this nigga funny as fuck. Watch how he look at you when he get over here."

"What's going on, Brother Kashmir and sista?" He stuck his hand out to Heaven as he lustfully looked her up and down. She shook his hand and frowned. Although he was dressed nicely, he still had a hood twang in his voice and a bop in his walk.

"Heaven," Kash said as he pulled Heaven's hand from Rocky's.

"Oh, my apologies."

"It's cool, G." Kash tapped Pastor Rocky's chest.
"This is my baby." He introduced. "You good, baby?"He looked down at Heaven.

"Yeah, I'm fine."

"Where did Lance and Esha run off to? I needed to talk to him about joining the church."

"Oh, Lance and Esha went to Mrs. Roberts's crib. You should stop by and holla at him. Before we saw you, he was saying something about joining." Kash smirked mischievously.

"I will... But while I got you here, I wanted to talk to you about visiting Holy Cross of Christ as well. You know we can all use the word of God in our lives."

"Nah, Pastor. That shi..." Kash began to curse, forgetting he was talking to a man of the cloth, but quickly recanted his words. He smirked and licked his lips as Pastor Rocky frowned, raising one brow. "I mean, church ain't for me." He took a sip from his cup.

"Why not? The Lord," his voice galloped loudly, feeling the spirits take over his body and deliverance, causing Heaven to jump and look up at Kash, "loves us all. We are all his children. Ain't that right, Sista

Heaven?"

"Uhm, yeah, I... I guess."

"You know your parents gave you that name for a reason. You were put on this earth to serve the Lord. The church is where you belong. Now, of course, you wouldn't be able to dress this provocatively, but a beautiful pair of slacks or appropriate dress will suffice."

Kash laughed while Heaven looked at him confusingly.

"Pastor Rocky, Sista Heaven and I are atheist. We believe there is a higher power, but all that church and Christ shit... I mean, my bad." Kash shook his head.
"All that church stuff, we can't fuck with it."

"Brother Kashmir, you need the Lord. All that foul language, my brother, isn't called for."

"Hey, Killa!" a couple of girls said as they walked past.

"What's up?" he said to the ladies before responding to Rocky. "Nigga, cut all that reverend shit out. I saw that Kirk Franklin video. You mafuckas be cussing niggas out. Plus, yo' sanctified ass is from the hood."

"Kashmir, my brother, my past life does not dictate who I am today. My past is behind me. What you see right now is the real me. Reborn and in the flesh. Giving all you lost souls the word was my calling."

Kash sighed and took a sip from his cup. Rocky was a known ex drug dealer, so him walking around the hood, preaching, had niggas like Kash feeling a little sketchy.

"That's what's up, Rocky. I can't even knock what you got going on. It's all love, my nigga. Or is it my preacher?" Kash asked, raising a hand to shake Rocky's. They embraced. "Either way, me and shorty ain't gon' be able to make it to Sunday service."

"Well, will you at least consider it? Maybe we can change your mind."

"There's nothing to consider." Kash took a sip from his cup. "I stand firm on how I feel. But I will make a nice contribution to the church, bro."

"I appreciate that, Kashmir. Thank you, brother." They shook hands again.

"Yeah, I know, but me and Sista Heaven gotta get outta here. One of my lil' cousins performing tonight."

"Alright, talk to you later, Brother Kashmir and Sista Heaven."

"See you." Heaven smiled, wrapping her arm around Kash's waist before walking off.

TWELVE

"G, you bogus as hell for leaving me like that. But we on the porch." Hanging up the phone, Kash looked at Heaven. "I told you that nigga was funny as hell," Kash said as they approached Mrs. Roberts's steps. "All I had to tell that nigga was I was going to donate to his church, and I knew he would shut the fuck up."

"He was a little weird though, and I didn't like the way he kept looking at me." Heaven took a seat on a yellow chair that sat on the porch and placed one leg on top of the other one, crossing them at the knee.

"Can you blame him?" Kash rubbed his beard.

The skintight, beige, off-white tube top dress she had on had Kash staring at her. He looked at her from her head to her toes, noting everything about her, from her now crinkling hair, the gold, eighteen-inch Heaven necklace around her neck, her braless breasts, and protruding hips. Looking at her fingers that were now intertwined at her knees, he looked at how perfectly her nails were painted, so he looked down at her feet just to make sure they were just as equally perfect, which he knew they were. Kash couldn't help but to look at her admirably. She was the shit, and she carried herself well. She was sexy in every way imaginable.

"What?" she smiled, "What's up? You're looking at me all weird and shit like your pastor friend." Kash looked at how perfect her lips and teeth were, and he licked his lips.

"My pastor friend can't do to you the shit I can." He took a seat on the chair next to her and laid the back of his head on her breast. Looking up at her, he touched her mink lashes and then her lips.

"And what's that?" she asked, reciprocating Kash's touches. She ran her fingers through his beard and cocked her head to the side, looking him in his eyes. He didn't respond. He just chuckled.

Looking into Heaven's eyes, he thought about her conversation with Kamelia earlier that day. He wasn't eavesdropping, but he paid attention to the way Heaven conversed with his daughter. Her vocabulary was very nurturing. Using words like pretty and beautiful were for sure a boost to Kamelia's self-esteem. Even how she effortlessly told Kamelia she loved her did something to Kash. Unlike a lot of women, Heaven didn't misuse and abuse his daughter because he walked away. She seemed to be patient and attentive, and he knew she wasn't just doing it for show. This had to be who Heaven was on the regular.

Hearing Kamelia reciprocate and speak back to Heaven, without fear in her voice, made Kash love and appreciate Heaven even more.

"Man, what the fuck y'all out here doing?" Lance asked as he opened the screen door with a lit blunt in his hand. "This shit cute and all, but come on, G, blow this weed with me."

"Right. Y'all can finish loving on each other after we smoke." Slamming the screen door, Esha stood in front of Heaven and Kash with one hand on her hip and her other hand up to her mouth, holding the blunt while she puffed on it. She waited for Kash to get up so that she could sit down.

However, Kash didn't get up. He just pulled Heaven up by her hand and sat her on his lap. He hugged her around her stomach and laid his head on her back.

"Sucka ass," Lance said, laughing.

Putting the blunt in rotation, Esha passed it to Lance and poured herself a cup of liquor.

"Do you smoke, Heaven?" Esha asked curiously, putting her cup to her lips.

"Not really."

"Not really? What type of answer is that? You either do or you don't, suga."

"Yes, Esha, I smoke sometimes. It's not my drug of choice, but I will hit the weed from time to time."

"What is your drug of choice?" Kash asked, curiously. "Before you answer that, it better not be no off the wall crackhead shit."

"I don't know why I said it like that because I don't have a drug of choice to begin with, but I pop pills occasionally. Depending on the situation."

Kash sat back in his seat and looked at Heaven. He didn't like her answer. And now that he was back in her life, he was going to make sure popping pills were a thing of the past.

"Oh, okay! I guess it's not worse than weed."

"It is," Kash said. "G, don't touch a pill while you're around me."

"I don't plan to."

The weed was passed to Kash. He took a pull from it. Turning Heaven around to look at him, he pulled her face to his, pressed his lips against hers, and blew the smoke into her mouth.

Heaven took the shotgun like a G, instantly feeling the effects of the weed. Like she said, she didn't really smoke, so goosebumps gathered on her arms, and her body began to feel a little loose. She smiled widely and turned to look at Esha, who was staring out into the front yard with a goofy expression on her face. Heaven burst out into an obnoxious laughter as Kash handed her the weed. Esha turned to look at her.

"What's so damn funny? I know you're not high already."

"No." She lied. "You just look funny as hell right now."

"Girl, fuck you. This some good ass weed."

Heaven took a couple pulls before passing the blunt to Esha.

As Esha put the brown leafy paper to her mouth, the sound of a horn blowing and a woman's voice yelling took them from their weed session. Simultaneously, they all turned their heads in the direction of the car that sat idle, parked directly in front of Lance's mother's house.

Instantly, Esha put the blunt out and stood. How dare this bitch, Asia, pull up in front of her mother-in-law's house, blowing her horn like she ran some shit?

"Aye, G." Lance tapped Kash's arm as Esha began to walk down the stairs.

"G, where the fuck you going?" He grabbed her arm and pulled her back up the stairs, already knowing what Esha was prepared to do.

"What is she doing here, Kashmir?"

"How the fuck would I know?" He frowned.

"Nah uhn, nigga. Don't talk to my friend like that."

"Esha, shut the fuck up."

"Right, Kash. I don't give a fuck if you're mad right now. Don't talk to me like that. I'm not one of these little simple minded, dumb ass bitches."

"I never called you dumb or simple minded. I been with yo' ass ever since yesterday. I haven't talked to Asia since the basketball game. How would I know why she's here?" Kash sat up and put his hand to Heaven's face, gripping her chin, forcing her to look at him.

"Kash!" Asia yelled again.

"Come on. Let's go see what she wants." Heaven stood up, but Kash pulled her back down on his lap.

"What I tell you earlier? Fuck her."

"Well, I'ma hit that bitch in her fucking mouth. Watch." Esha threatened.

"No, you're not. You are gonna mind your own business. Kash don't fuck with Asia, bro. She just tryna stir up some bullshit."

"Man, fuck her. Shorty crazy as fuck. She ain't worth the drama."

"Lance, tell your friend to come here."

"Bitch, don't say my nigga's name no more."

Lance just shook his head, laughed, and looked at Kash.

"She must really want her ass whooped. You better tell her about me, Kash."

"Man, Esha, leave that shit alone. Just ignore her."

So, they all did just that. Asia wasn't crazy enough to get out her car and step foot on Lance's mother's porch, so all she could do was blow her horn and call Kash's name until it became old and worn out.

She put her vehicle in drive, but before she drove away, she said, "You must really want me to die, Kashmir. I told you I can't live without you, and I meant that."

***

After spending an hour or so on Mrs. Roberts's porch, the four made their way to the big field where over a hundred people stood around, surrounding the small stage, watching the talents as they performed. After their conversation with Rocky, Heaven was a little annoyed, but now that she was a little intoxicated, she was feeling a lot better. Even with envious eyes watching her every move, Heaven was zoned out. She stood side by side with Esha, while Kash and Lance stood behind them, in the front of the crowded park at the stage, hugged up. They danced and moved to the slow music while a group of girls and boys danced provocatively on stage. Her mouth was wide open though. The sight was crazy to Heaven. These were kids that couldn't be any more than twelve years old. The little girls were hip rolling and rubbing their little behinds on the little boys in front of their parents and the entire community. Nevertheless, the crowd was cheering them on.

"Back in the day, this used to be my little fast ass on this same stage, dancing and poking my lil' skinny ass booty out on these little boys' peter weter," Esha said, yelling over the music.

"Eeww! I wish Kamelia would. That'll be her very first ass whipping."

"If Kamelia is anything like you, she wouldn't dare."

"Period!"

Soon after the group finished dancing, a local comedian came on stage and told a few jokes that had the crowd laughing out loud, literally.

"And look at Killa with this light skinned, delectable, sexy shorty... Hey, mamacita!" the comedian said, waving at Heaven.

"Aye, my nigga, watch yo' mouth."

"Naw, Killa. I wasn't gon' say shit disrespectful. I know how you get down, but I see you out here looking like the light skinned member of a R&B group. You hugging on shorty like a dark skinned nigga gon' slide in and steal her." He cracked, and everyone laughed, including Kash and Heaven. They were high as fuck, and the comedian was on a roll with the jokes. "Aye, G, you don't have to feel threatened by me... Shorty, blink twice if you're being held hostage by this Al B. Sure looking ass nigga."

After the comedian, a rapper named Jay Beezie and his two hype men graced the stage. Their look was on point from their groomed fades and facial hair to what they wore on their bodies. They looked like three rich niggas who didn't need the music industry to make money because they already had it. They were from the neighborhood and were recently signed to a huge record company. The beat for their music was on point and so were their lyrics. With great crowd participation, everyone knew the lyrics to his song.

This was who Kash came all the way to the front of the stage to see. His little cousin, Jay Beezie. He was like a proud big cousin as he nodded his head and rapped along.

"Aye, lil cuz talking his shit!" Lance screamed over the music as he bopped his head as well.

"For sho. That lil' nigga be going crazy, G."

"On my mama."

After Jay's performance, he joined Kash down in the crowd and politicked with him for a little while. As the night went on, the excitement began to calm down, but when the last act was introduced, and the instrumental to Best Part by H.E.R. featuring Daniel Cesar began to play, the crowd cheered loudly. Two girls walked on the stage and began singing, taking turns with the verses and chorus.

Heaven turned around and hugged Kash around his waist as he wrapped his arms around her shoulders. She laid her head on his chest, and together, they swayed, rocking along to the beat. This was the perfect song to end the show. Being intoxicated had Heaven in her feelings. As she laid wrapped up in Kash's embrace, she thought about her life at home with Derrick. In all honesty, their relationship wasn't bad, but her heart was no longer in it. She couldn't even say with confidence if her heart was ever in it. Nostalgia was not in her heart for Derrick as she stood here with Kash. Being with him just felt so right.

THIRTEEN

"Y'all were just too cute back there," Esha said to Heaven. Holding hands, Heaven and Esha leaned on each other for support while they cackled like little hens as they walked back to the parking lot she parked Kash's car in earlier. Of course, Kash and Lance walked directly behind the women, making sure they all made it back to the car safe and sound.

Neither Kash nor Lance were into kicking it in the hood all night. They had their women with them, and the hood tended to get a little dangerous after a certain time. It was ten in the evening and time for Kash to get Heaven home. He needed to be alone after the long day he had, needing to get to the forest preserve to sort out his thoughts. He didn't plan on going to see Asia; however, he did plan to call her and talk to her. Asia wanting to kill herself because of him didn't sit well. He didn't take Asia's words lightly; he knew she was mentally unstable. Although he no longer dealt with her in a romantic way, he still cared about her well-being. He didn't want her to hurt herself just because he didn't want to be with her. But he wasn't about to be miserable just so she could be happy.

They all climbed into the car, and Kash pulled off. They rode silently as the music played through the stereo, and Kash drove out the parking lot. Minutes later, they were getting on the expressway. He drove in the direction of downtown Chicago to drop Heaven off at home first before he took the ride up north to drop Lance and Esha off.

"I'ma drop you off first, baby."

"No, you're not," she slurred. "I'm going home with you. I got my overnight bag in the trunk, or after you drop them off, we can go back to my apartment. Either way, I need you tonight."

"All that sappy shit," Esha slurred from the backseat, and Kash turned the music up a little.

"I got something I need to do tonight. I can come back to yo' crib when I'm done if you want me to."

With a scowl on her face, Heaven looked at Kash.

"Kashmir, I don't care what you need to do. I'm goingwith you."

He scratched his head and blew out a breath. He was cool with her going with him. He had nothing to hide from her, and he knew she thought he had plans to go see Asia. So, to put her mind at ease, he gave in to her demands. Driving past her exit, he merged onto the Kennedy Expressway. Fifteen minutes later, they were pulling up in front of Esha's house, directly across the street from the home Reign grew up in.

It was as if Asia was watching Kash's every move because as soon as he pulled into the driveway, his phone began to ring. Looking down at it, he sent her to voicemail. He stepped out the car with his phone ringing nonstop in his hand while Lance and Esha got out as well.

"See you later, boo." Esha hugged Heaven through the window and quickly walked to her front door. She was tired and ready to call it a night.

Meanwhile, Kash and Lance stood on the opposite side of the car to talk. The entire time, Kash's cell still vibrated in his hand. Something had to be wrong, or Asia was having another mental moment. He didn't want to answer the phone, but something in him told him that something was very wrong. Kash showed his phone screen to Lance and shook his head.

"Stay right here for a minute while I answer this." Not wanting to answer his phone for Asia in front of Heaven, and not wanting to look suspicious just standing outside, he picked up. Before he could even say hello, Malaysia's crying voice pierced his ear alarmingly.

"Kash!" she cried.

"Yeah, what's wrong?"

"It's Mama. She is dead I think."

"Wait, wait. What do you mean?" Kash's concern was evident in his voice and facial expression. He was frowned up, almost in tears, but he stayed calm for the sake of Asia's six year old daughter, who was smart enough to call for help.

"I went in her room to ask her for Taiwan pampers, and she was in the bed, under the covers. I thought she was sleep. So, I pulled the cover off her face, and she wasn't breathing a lot."

"Okay, Malaysia, calm down. Where is she now?"

"I called the police, and they sent the ambulance. They are in her bedroom right now with her. We're scared they are going to take us."

"Aight," Kash sighed. "Don't be scared. I'm on my way over there." He hung up.

"What happened?"

"This fucking girl really tried…" Kash stopped in the middle of his statement and pinched the bridge of his nose with his thumb and index finger.

"Who? Asia?"

"Yeah, that was her daughter. She said Asia wasn't breathing when she went in her bedroom. I gotta go over there and make sure the kids are good."

"Man, what if Asia crazy ass set this whole thing up, knowing you would run over there to see about her kids? Heaven gon' fuck you up."

"I know. I can't even think straight right now. The least I can do is go check, just to make sure shit is good. Do you mind taking her home?"

"You know I got you, G. What you gon' tell Heaven though?"

"Taking who home? Tell me about what?" Heaven asked, walking around the car to get in his face. Minutes prior, after wondering what was taking Kash so long to get back in the car, Heaven got out. She heard his entire conversation with Malaysia, and she knew what happened to Asia. However, it wasn't his job to play daddy to her kids.

"So, you about to go to Asia's house and do what? You're not her kids' fucking daddy. It's not your job to look after them because her weak ass don't know how to deal with life and put her kids first. Why are they calling you anyways? She doesn't have family to go get her kids? Where the hell is her baby daddy? Call him."

"I agree, Heaven. But I wouldn't want to see anything bad happen to her kids because of a mistake she made. Lance, can you take her home?"

"I don't need nobody to take me the fuck home. I don't need this shit, Kash. You clearly still want to fuck with her. So, fuck you. And fuck you too, Lance."

Heaven walked off in the direction of the twins' home, and Kash ran up behind her.

"Man, where the fuck are you going?"

"Get your damn hands off me, Kash." She looked up at him. She was beyond pissed. She knew he still had feelings for Asia. "I'm going to my stepmom brothers' house."

"G, you disrespectful as fuck, but I'ma let you go. I can't deal with your little temper tantrum right now." He let her arm go, and she walked away.

***

Calling Reign's brother Bryson's phone while ringing the doorbell, Heaven was in tears. All the lights were off, even the lights in the front of the house, and one car sat in the driveway. She was intoxicated and pissed the hell off at Kash's choice to leave her while he went and checked on another bitch, leaving her to be someone else's responsibility. And she was mad at Lance just because. He was Kash's friend, and in her heart, she knew he encouraged Kash's behavior. She didn't smoke, but she wished she had a cigarette right now.

"I can't believe this shit," Heaven said. She wanted to call her father but quickly thought better of it. She was an adult and had to deal with her own grownup problems. Plus, she knew that maybe she was being a little selfish. Asia possibly committing suicide had to be fucking with Kash's mental. Still, Heaven didn't care. Asia was weak for ever contemplating taking her own life over a nigga. The dick was good, but it wasn't that good.

After not getting an answer from Bryson or Byron, she decided she would just take a Lyft home because she refused to walk back across the street to Esha's house. She wouldn't give Kash the satisfaction of her allowing his friend to take her home. So, she sat on the steps and ordered a $150 Lux ride. The entire time she sat there, she cried. It didn't take long. Two minutes later, her ride pulled up, and she slowly stood from the step. She knew her dress was dirty and ruined, but she didn't care. She didn't plan to wear it again anyway. Plus, her heart was torn to pieces, and that was the only thing that mattered to her right now. She opened the door and climbed inside, sulking as she sat down on the leather seats.

"Heaven Wright?"

"Yes!"

Closing her eyes, she felt the truck take off down the street. In no time, they were pulling up in front of her building.

Heaven couldn't wait until she made it home. At the front door, she stripped from her clothes and poured herself a cup of Remy. Afterwards, she got in the shower and broke down crying. She didn't know if she was being overly dramatic, but shit, her heart was on fire. In her mind, Kash made up an excuse just to see Asia, and he was at her house, playing family man once again.

Sliding down the wall with her sudsy towel pressed to her chest, she let the water pour on her. Her face was soaked and wet from both water and her tears. This wasn't like her. She never cried over a man. Kash was the only man that made her cry. This wasn't the first time, but as she hurt in the shower, she promised herself it would be the last.

Little did she know, Kash honestly could care less about Asia. He loved Heaven. He had showed her the most intimate parts of his life. He had given her intimacy. He didn't have to make up an excuse to see her. If he wanted to be with Asia, he would be. It was that simple. He was just a good person who blamed himself for Asia's unfortunate situation. However, Heaven was too trapped in her rage to see that. She felt what she felt.

When she reached the floor, she sat there for a while, feeling dumb. She had everything in life, but here she was, crying over a nigga who would prefer to run to a broke bitch's rescue. Asia had nothing to bring to any table Kash sat at.

Heaven stood up and wiped her eyes. She quickly washed up and rinsed off. After she stepped from the shower, she took her shower cap off, went into her bedroom, put on her pajamas, and went into the living room. She retrieved her glass of Remy and the dress she had on before holding it up in her hand and tossing it in the garbage. She sighed and walked over to the couch, took a seat, turned the TV to a music video channel, and turned it up.

Tonight, she was in her feelings, and although she was done crying, she needed the world to know how she felt about Kashmir Harris. Picking up her phone, she clicked on her Facebook app, and the first thing she saw was a picture of Kamelia and Regan with their dolls on Reign's Facebook page. She smiled, hearted the picture, and then scrolled back up. This pretty picture of her daughter and little sister was not going to stop her from exposing how Kash just broke her heart for Asia. No one on her page knew who Kash was besides Esha and Reign, still she was about to talk her shit. She pressed the live button.

With the R&B music playing and a cup of liquor in her hand, she was in her zone. She'd always come off as perfect, but the sight of her with her face red and her eyes puffy from crying didn't look so perfect. She looked like a normal human being.

"So, I'm in the Chi in this pretty ass apartment my daddy got for me. The view is so fucking amazing, y'all. All these tall buildings and beautiful lighting has had me in awe since I arrived." As she talked, she saw a few people begin to tune in. Esha was one and a few other people from her high school and college. Putting the phone closer to her face, she read a comment from Esha, asking why her face was so red.

"Esha, it's a long story, but ask Lance. He knows why. I can't believe I ran my ass all the way to Chicago to reunite with Kashmir, just to be dis-re-fucking-spected." She took a sip from her cup. "You know, as a mother, you want your kids to know their entire family. Just so shit won't be weird when they get older. At least for me, I want my daughter to know where she comes from and who her father is, but damn, sometimes it's best to just let certain shit be. It doesn't matter if you're in love with that person. If y'all missed out on years of being with each other then let it be and keep it moving. Don't rekindle shit. Don't let that nigga fuck you. Don't let him play in your cat." She laughed, but she was serious. "Because that leaves room for him to play with your heart. Bitch, I know the dick be good. I know you may have missed it over the years, but trust me, that sex is toxic."

Heaven's phone began to ring which caused an interruption in her live video. She looked at the name and saw it was Reign calling her, so she quickly rejected the call and continued with her video. She was no longer reading the comments, so she could only imagine what people were thinking, and she could only imagine the look on Reign's face as she watched her talk about dick and sex. But talking about it was starting to help her feel better. She took another sip from her cup and sighed.

"Ma, I'ma call you back. Let me talk my shit real quick because Kashmir Harris got me fucked up." She pulled her hair behind her ears. Her eyes were low, and her words were slurred as she pursed her lips, snaked her neck, and pointed her long fingernails into the camera. "This nigga wanna be Captain Save A Hoe, running behind a suicidal ass bitch because she threaten to kill herself if he don't want to be with her. I can't stand a weak ass hoe, and his ass is just as weak for ever dealing with a girl of her caliber. I won't even cap. She is a beautiful girl or whatever, but she is dumb as fuck. She has three kids but want to kill herself over some dick," she said, frowning into the camera. "Make it make sense, sis. You have to be a weird, sick individual to threaten your own life over a nigga. Admittedly, the dick is magnificent, but I'm not about to leave my daughter on this earth alone over it. Fuck that!"

Putting her glass to her lips and taking a sip, she put the phone closer to her face, deciding she would read Reign's comment.

Hey, Pooh, you need to get off live. You're intoxicated. You need to sleep on these feelings. What you're saying is none of Facebook's business.

"I hear you, Ma, but I am so pissed right now. You know I don't do this Facebook stuff. Kashmir really tried me like I'm not a rich bitch who can bring my own shit to a relationship. Still, he chooses to run behind a bum bitch with no money or anything to show that she is a real woman besides the three little fuckers she pushed out her sour ass pussy."

Hearing the front door open, Heaven continued her live video. She knew it was Kash, but she didn't care. She was going to finish her video, cuss him the fuck out, and then move on with her life.

"And anybody that knows me knows I don't talk bad about anybody's kids, but this nigga got me bent! He's lucky I love his ass because if I didn't, I would've sent my daddy and uncle at him."

***

When Kash pulled up on Asia's block, he was a little confused by how quiet it was outside. He didn't really know what to expect but because Malaysia told him the ambulance was there with Asia, he kind of thought the block would be lit up with police, fire trucks, ambulances, and possibly even a coroner's car. However, no one was out there.

He parked across the street from her house and got out. Slamming the door, he pressed the alarm and made his way across the street and up to her front door. He twisted the doorknob, just to see if the door was unlocked, and it was. He walked inside and into the living room. Everything still looked intact. It was spotless, calm, and quiet, with the exception of the television that was on and turned up high. All three kids were asleep. India and Taiwan were knocked out on the sofa while Malaysia was sleep on the loveseat. Kash frowned, confused by the entire scene. If the ambulance had really been there and found Asia unresponsive, they would've removed the kids when they took her body for sure.

He walked over to the loveseat, knelt, and woke Malaysia up. "Malaysia, wake up." He shook her.

"Huh?"

"Wake up." Kash stood and picked Malaysia up. He sat on the couch and sat her on his lap.

Malaysia laid her head on Kash's shoulder and hugged him around his neck.

"Wake up. What happened?"

"I'm sorry," she whispered. "Mama made me do it."

"Do what?"

"She made me call you over here. She was sad when she came home, and she told me to call you but tell you she wasn't breathing."

Kash scowled and grunted. This had to be the lowest shit any female had pulled on him. It was crazy how she used her child, knowing Kash was attached to them, to lure him over there.

"Where is she?"

"She's in her room."

"Aight." He stood up and laid Malaysia back down on the loveseat. "You're okay, right?"

"Yes."

"Okay, give me a hug. If you need anything, no matter the time of day, call me. Okay?"

"Okay." Malaysia smiled.

Kash was so done with Asia. He decided to just leave and cut all ties with Asia, even his relationship with her kids. Heaven was right. He wasn't their father, and it was crazy how she used her kids, kids he shouldn't have any emotional ties to, to play with his emotions.

He left her home and her life, ready to move forward with Heaven and Kamelia.

As he walked back to his car, he heard Asia calling his name, but he never looked back. Instead, he tried calling Heaven's phone, got in his car, started it up, and pulled off. After she didn't answer, he assumed she blocked him. Initially, he planned to go to the forest preserve to clear his mind, but he didn't want Heaven to be worried. Plus, he felt bad, so he drove all the way back to Park Ridge to pick her up and take her home. Pulling into the driveway of the home he watched Heaven walk to earlier, he got out, went up to the door, and rang the doorbell. He knew Heaven was pissed at him, but he was coming back to get his woman. He stood there for ten minutes, ringing the doorbell repeatedly, but when no one answered, he got back into his car and called Lance.

"Yo," Lance said groggily into the phone.

"Aye, bro, ask Esha do she know where Heaven went."

"Hold on. Esha!"

"Yes, babe. You're gonna wake the baby up."

"Aye, you know where Heaven is?"

"She's with Kash. Isn't she?"

"No, she went across the street earlier when Killa told her he had to make a quick run."

Esha sucked her teeth and turned around to look at Lance. "What the fuck happened, Lance and Kash? Where is my friend?" She sat up in bed, grabbed her phone, and called Heaven's number; however, she didn't answer. Something told Esha to log onto Facebook, and she did just that. Her notifications told her Heaven was live, and when she clicked on the live, she looked at Heaven curiously. Her music was loud, and she looked worn out, like she had a rough night. "It looks like she went home," Esha announced.

"Bro, shorty on live right now, looking crazy as hell, like she been crying and drinking."

"Let me ask my friend what's wrong because, Kash, if you hurt her, I'ma fuck you up." She began typing, pressing send. Heaven instantly responded.

"Man, let me go check on her. Thank you, G." He could only imagine what Heaven's live was about. Although he wasn't into the whole social media thing, he knew people loved to use Facebook as a way to validate their point of view.

Kash hung up and did at least fifty on the streets and about eighty on the expressway. It didn't take him long, but when he finally reached Heaven's building, he pulled into the parking lot and parked next to her truck that she had yet to drive. It had been sitting in the same exact spot for weeks now, and dust was starting to form on the hood and roof. He made a mental note to take it through a carwash to get it cleaned.

He walked into the building from the parking garage and walked over to the elevator. Pressing the button, it felt like forever before the elevator reached the lobby. The bell dinged, and he stepped on with his head hung low. He didn't really knowing what part of Heaven he was getting ready to walk in on, but he was ready to deal with it. As the elevator reached the eighth floor, the bell dinged again. The door opened, and he stepped out. Walking up to her front door, he reached atop the panel and pulled the spare key down. As soon as he unlocked the door, he heard Heaven's voice, going off about him and Asia.

Kash turned the corner and walked over to Heaven. He snatched the phone from her hand.

"Man, why the fuck you putting Facebook in our business?" He looked into the phone and smirked at the comments that were on the screen.

Heaven sat back on the couch with her cup of Remy in her hand and cradled a decorative pillow in between her legs.

Kash pressed 'End Live' and threw her phone on the couch, right on the side of her. He stood there, staring at her as her phone began to vibrate. With accusatory eyes, he frowned as she picked it up.

"That bet not be that nigga."

"Kash, fuck you, okay? You and that half dead ass bitch you just went to go check on." Heaven rolled her eyes at him.

Kash smirked. "Yeah, okay!" He took his shirt off and began to walk to the kitchen, as if everything was cool between them, but Heaven was on his ass. She lifted the pillow, cocked it back, and threw it at him. She stood up and rushed him but quickly backed down when he turned around with a serious expression on his face and his fist balled, ready to yoke her up.

Flinching, she backed up, away from him. "What the fuck... You was about to hit me?"

"Nah, I will never hit you, shorty, but I will choke the fuck outta you if you don't keep your hands to yourself."

"Fuck you, Kashmir." She walked up on him again, grabbing at his pant pockets. "Give me my house key. You come up in here, taking your shirt off like you're here to stay when you can really get the fuck out. I'm done with your stupid ass."

"Jo, get the fuck up off me." He pushed her back. "I'm not giving you shit. This my mufuckin' key."

"No, it's not, Kash." Again, she walked in his face. "Give me my shit! You left me outside, in a fucking city I know absolutely nothing about, to go check on the next bitch."

"Bro, I didn't leave you alone. I asked Lance to bring you home. You chose to take your stubborn ass across the street, and I wasn't about to chase after you."

"But you can chase after her? Kamelia should be your number one priority, no one else. So, give me my fuckin' key, and get the fuck out, Kashmir."

"Man, you better go sit your short ass down somewhere. I'm not giving you shit, and I'm not going nowhere." He picked her up, and she poked her bottom lip out as she folded her arms across her chest defiantly. "You didn't let me explain or shit. You just so ready to get me outta your life."

"Kash, put me down." Her voice was low and tired.

"Nah!" He carried her over to the couch and sat down with her still in his arms.

"Why not? There is nothing you need to explain to me." She stood from his lap. "Your actions are enough for me. You're playing father of the year in a household that doesn't belong to you while me and your real blood daughter is pushed to the fucking side. What else is there you need to explain? Tell me, Kash. Tell me, so I can understand. What the hell do you need to explain?"

"Baby, please just come here. Calm down. I told you this before, and I'm promising you that I don't give a fuck about Asia." He sat up and reached for Heaven's hand. Pulling her to him, he hugged her around her waist and looked up at her. "You know the shit I've been through with my mama, so when it came to Asia's kids, I had a soft spot in my heart for them because the way Asia treats them is fucked up. Jo, I can relate, and I just felt like it was my job to go check on them when Malaysia called me saying she found Asia unresponsive."

"Why was that your job, Kash?"

"It just was. I'm not a heartless person." He released her and sat back. "Her daughter sounded scared as fuck, and the protector in me forced me over there. I did what I would want someone to do for our daughter in that same situation."

"Kamelia will never be in that situation. Do you really think I will kill myself over you?"

"That's not even the point, Heaven. I would've taken you with me, but I didn't want to pull you into my bullshit."

"And I would've went with you. Bullshit or not, we can't call ourselves being in a relationship if you don't respect me enough to include me in the decisions you make. How do I know you didn't make up an excuse to go over there and fuck her?"

"G, I don't have to make an excuse for shit I do. I didn't fuck her. I didn't even see her, and I'm not about to stand here and argue with you about her." Folding his arms across his chest, he continued. "I'm not used to this relationship shit. I move how I move, and I don't feel like I need to explain myself..."

Heaven cut him off. "You don't have to explain yourself. You're a grown ass man." The left side of Heaven's lip curled upwards. She was being condescending. Kash knew he was a grown ass man. Still, if they were going to be together, he did have to explain himself. Sitting up, he wrapped an arm around her legs.

"Heaven, bro, stop talking over me. Let me finish saying what the fuck I need to say," he said, and she was silent. "I'm willing to explain myself to you. You just gotta trust me. And I'm sorry for making you feel like I don't give a fuck."

"You don't give a fuck." Heaven rolled her eyes and removed Kash's arms from around her. "Where are her kids now? Did the bitch even try to kill herself?"

"Her kids are at home." He stood up and walked back to the kitchen while Heaven followed behind him. "The whole thing was a setup. She told her daughter to call me. When I got there, they were sleep, and I assume Asia was in her room. I didn't go past the living room. Malaysia told me the truth, and I left. I don't want shit to do with her. And although I'm not heartless, I know I have to let her kids go too. I'm just ready to get to Baby K. I need to see her."

"Don't try to use my baby to fill your little void, Kash."

"Never that. Heaven, stop playing with me." He turned around and grabbed her by her pajama shirt. "No one will ever mean more to me than my daughter. I know I fucked up in the past. I missed a huge portion of her life, but that shit is the past. I'm tired of hearing about it. I'm here now. Stop throwing that shit in my face."

"Okay, Kash."

"And don't take your crazy ass back on Facebook, telling people our business. I don't know what you're used to, nor do I care, but I'm a grown ass man, and I don't do shit like that. We have to be on the same page, baby."

FOURTEEN

The Following Week

Removing her Air Pods from her ears, she looked over at Kash, who was knocked out sleep right on the side of her.

"Welcome to my city, boo!" Leaning over, she whispered in his ear and kissed his cheek to wake him up.

"We made it here quick as hell." Stretching, Kash sat up and looked out the window.

This was Heaven's plan from the beginning. She had gone to Chicago with an agenda. Heaven didn't know if Kash would accept her in his life, but she was happy she took a chance. Now, their relationship was to the point of making introductions. Finally, Heaven was ready for Kash to meet Kamelia and Sno. They were the only two people whose opinions mattered to her when it came to her making life changing decisions.

She had left everything she took to Chicago back in Chicago, hoping that her baby and father approved of Kash. If they did, she was taking Kamelia and going back home to Chicago, at least for another month or two. They were still trying to build their relationship.

Heaven smiled, looking out the window as the plane slowly descended from the sky, and the wheels came down from underneath the plane. Excitement filled her. She was ready for Kash to experience the place she was raised. It was not just the city but the home and loving atmosphere her father provided her with.

They were only staying in Atlanta for two days. So, Kash only brought a duffle bag of clothes and shoes, something casual and something comfortable. Today, they were having dinner with Sno and Reign, and then tomorrow, they planned to hang out before going back to Chicago.

Standing up, Kash retrieved his bag from the overhead compartment and stood to the side, allowing Heaven to walk in front of him as they exited the plane. He wrapped his arm around her shoulder and walked down the long ramp. "You need me to order an Uber or one of your chauffeurs coming to pick us up?"

"I don't have any chauffeurs, silly." She laughed.
"We're taking an Uber." Pulling her purse on her shoulder and intertwining her fingers with Kash's, they walked through the airport.

Heaven coming home today was a surprise, even to her. Nobody knew she was coming back home today. At the last minute, Kash booked them a flight and told her the night before that they were leaving first thing in the morning. So, here they were, walking through Hartsfield-Jackson International, looking like a beautiful couple.

Heaven put Sno and Reign's address, into her Uber app. The prices to get to their destination were super expensive; nevertheless, she ordered it. There were plenty of Uber and Lyft rides just sitting around, still their ride was ten minutes away.

Heaven smiled brightly as they made their way outside of the airport. With his back up against the glass, Heaven stood in front of him. He wrapped his arms around her waist, and she laid the back of her head on his chest. Heaven was ready to show Kash off to her family. She was happy.

As soon as their ride reached them, they got inside. With the heavy traffic, it took about an hour to reach Sno's home. They held hands, laughed, and held whispered conversations the entire way. Although they shared a five-year-old daughter together, their relationship was fairly new, and it was obvious. They seemed to be fascinated with one another, and it was from the way they looked into each other's eyes to the way a smile would grace their faces as they spoke in hushed tones. Their love seemed new. They were too old for puppy love; however, adoration was apparent.

This was grown up, adult love.

Heaven saw smoke coming from the backyard as they pulled up to the house. So, she already knew where everyone was. The two climbed from inside the Uber and walked to the front door. Twisting the doorknob, they walked inside, and Heaven instructed Kash to leave his bag by the front door, on a bench, next to a window.

Walking through the house, Kash looked around. He opened doors to closets, bedrooms, bathrooms, even the refrigerator as they passed through the kitchen. He was a hood nigga, and although his house was nice, it was nothing like the huge crib Heaven's parents owned.

"Kash, what are you doing?" Heaven laughed, watching as he grabbed a can of Sprite from the French door, black, stainless-steel refrigerator. He opened the can and took a sip.

"What you mean?"

"You up in here, opening up refrigerators and shit. Reign is going to kick your ass."

"Shit, I just flew a million miles with you. I'm thirsty as fuck."

Heaven opened the back door and walked out with Kash right behind her. He was so tall standing behind her that he looked like a tall ass tower.

The kids were in the pool with Reign, so they weren't paying attention.

However, right away, Sno looked up from the grill and saw them. He gestured his head in a what's up motion, seeing his sweet pea. He didn't have to wonder who the man was behind her for obvious reasons. He had sandy brown hair, sun kissed skin, and Kamelia's whole face. It was clear who Kashmir was. Clamping his spatula to the side of the grill, he closed the lid and wiped his hand on his apron, before strolling towards Heaven and Kash.

"How you doing, Mr. Wright?" Kash stuck out his hand when Sno approached them and their hands met in a tight grip.

"What's good?"

"Kashmir, this is the best father any girl could ask for, Mr. Wright, and Daddy, this is Kamelia's father, Kash."

"Nice to finally meet you, Kash. We most definitely need to have a man-to-man conversation."

Sno had a serious expression on his face as he looked Kash in his eyes. He wasn't trying to intimidate Kash, but he did feel a way about how Kash had left Heaven to fend for herself while she was pregnant with his baby, not to mention she was just a baby herself.

"I agree." Kash nodded his head, matching Sno's

countenance. He understood Sno's displeasure. Honestly, he hadn't even met Kamelia yet, but he was sure he would fuck any nigga up over her. No questions asked.

"But first," Heaven cut in, "give your favorite daughter a hug." Those words alone instantly put a smile on Sno's face, calming his spirit as he looked at Heaven and wrapped her up in an embrace. "I love you, Daddy. Be nice to him."

"I got you." Sno's deep voice softened a little. All his girls had that effect on him. He was definitely prepared to be very hard on Kash, the same way KeKe had done with Reign all those years ago, but tougher considering the circumstances. Kash had left his daughter to be a single mother, and Sno needed to understand why, but for Heaven, he would take it a little easy. "I love you too, Sweet Pea."

After their hug, Sno turned to the huge, in-ground pool while Heaven wrapped her arms around Kash.

"Are you ready to meet your daughter?" she asked, looking up at him.

Kash licked his lips, looking down at her. "I been ready."

"She's a little spoiled and has a smart mouth, but she is all yours."

"Aye, Reign, look who finally decided to come

home!"

"Daddy!" Heaven laughed, hitting Sno's arm.

Reign turned around as the three began to walk towards the pool. When they approached, Reign climbed from inside, and Heaven opened her mouth wide, surprised at how big Reign had gotten over the past few weeks.

"Ma, look at you. Them babies got you looking very pregnant. And your skin looks so flawless," Heaven said, hugging Reign tightly.

"Thank you, Heaven. We just found out we're having boys. So, you have two little brothers on the way." Heaven held Reign out at arm's length, excitement etched on her face. Right now, there were more girls than boys in their family, and two baby boys would even them out.

"Oh my God. Congratulations, Ma. What are you naming them?"

"Thank you, boo! Baby A's name is Dillion, and baby B is Dominick."

"Their names are so cute."

Reign looked at Kash and smiled. "So, this is the infamous Kashmir?"

"Infamous?" Sno smirked, questioning Reign's comment.

"It's an insider." She looked at Heaven and pursed her lips together.

"Nice to meet you, Mrs. Wright."

"Mmm, and he has manners. Okay now, Kashmir." Reign smiled. "Does Kamelia know he's here?"

"No." Kamelia was so busy playing with Regan and DJ with her goggles on, and they were probably so fogged up that she didn't even realize Heaven was there. "I'm about to surprise her right now."

Reign and Sno stood to the side. The sight of Kamelia made Kash's heart skip a beat. She had so much sandy brown hair on the top of her head. Her skin was just as sun kissed as his, and the smile on her face was familiar. She was perfect. Kamelia was gorgeous, and the way she laughed while she and Regan splashed water on DJ made Kash smile himself. He wanted to cry. He was seeing his only child in the flesh for the first time. He'd seen plenty pictures of her, but they couldn't compare to how this moment made him feel.

"Kamelia," Heaven yelled. She didn't have to call her name twice. Immediately, Kamelia looked up, removing her goggles from her eyes. She, along with Regan and DJ, swam over to them.

"Mama," Kamelia yelled.

"Hey, bae." Heaven and Kash walked over.

Kneeling, Kash pulled Kamelia from the pool. He stood straight up.

"What's up, Baby K?"

"Who is Baby K?" With her head cocked back and her hands positioned in front of her, she looked at Kash, her eyebrows furrowed curiously. It was like looking into a mirror.

"You look exactly like me... I'm sorry," he whispered. "I've missed a lot." Water dripped from Kamelia's body and swimming suit onto Kash's clothes, but none of that mattered. A few tears slid from his eyes, as he silently stared at Kamelia, and she wiped them away. Kash closed his eyes as Kamelia's tiny fingers caught a tear in the corner of his right eye. He laid his head on her shoulder and wept.

"It's not too late, Kash," Heaven said, having sympathy for him. "You're here now. You're able to make up for lost time now."

"Ma, why is he crying?"

Heaven didn't respond. She was too busy crying herself. She wrapped her arms around Kash and Kamelia. Looking up at the two, she was happy that they were finally meeting each other.

"Do you know who this is, Kamelia?"

"Uhm, yeah," she said, and everyone laughed.

Kash finally looked at her again, wiping his tears. Kamelia was his baby, and her smart mouth was proof of that. He knew she was going to grab a hold of his heart and control it.

"Who am I, Kamelia?"

"You're Mama's little friend," she said innocently, putting her index finger to his bottom lip. "Right, Mama?"

"No, my love. This is your father."

"Well, duh, Ma! Look at his hair and look at mine. They are both brown."

After finally introducing Kash and Kamelia, they spent the rest of the day hanging out in the backyard. Kash helped Sno barbecue while Heaven changed into a bathing suit and got into the pool with Reign and the kids. Everything felt so complete. Still, she needed to go home and break the news to Derrick that they were over, and he had to get out her house. She prayed he left without causing a big scene because it was over, and there was no talking her out of that decision. She still had love for him, but now, it was time for her to explore what she left behind in Chicago.

"I did not see this coming. I could've sworn Derrick said you guys were going to plan your wedding when you came back home."

"Ma, I haven't been happy with Derrick in a long

time. When I brought the idea of me going to Chicago to my daddy a few months back, I told him how miserable I was. I felt like Kash and I didn't give one another a real chance, and I was just passing time with Derrick. I would rather us leave this relationship and still be friends."

"How do you think Derrick is going to take this information?"

"I don't know. Derrick's a big boy though. He should be able to accept me moving on. I mean, he works for the family, so he would have to be cordial because he is still going to be around. Plus, I don't love Derrick. I love Kashmir."

"Well, child, I'm happy for you. I'm even more excited for Kamelia. Look at them. Kash over there with you father, pretending like he's paying attention, but Kamelia won't let him put her down. A father's love is like no other. I tell you."

"Don't I know it."

"I wish my dad was still alive." Reign became misty eyed and a little emotional. Heaven hugged her with one arm, leaning her head against Reign's.

Afterwards, Reign informed Heaven about the information she had relayed to Sno about Anika and Bully. She also told her that they hadn't gotten Delilah since. Reign missed Delilah. She had been around since Delilah was little, and she knew Sno missed her too, but his pride wouldn't allow him to feel.

"I called the paternity court show," Reign said, looking at Heaven.

"Now, how did you get Mr. Wright to agree to that?"

"I haven't told him yet, but we need to get this test done. I know it's killing him. The fact that he doesn't know if she is or isn't. And then, with him not wanting to be around Delilah right now, I feel like that show was my only option. Plus, you know how your mama is. She would do anything for attention. So, I know a TV show will be right up her alley."

They sat there, talking and catching up, but the entire thing about her father going on a paternity show weighed heavily on Heaven's mind. Anika was an embarrassment, and she knew this entire thing would have Sno looking stupid in the end.

Meanwhile, Kash stood in front of the grill with Kamelia still in his arms. She was now lying on his chest while he and Sno had a general conversation. Not really wanting to say too much in front of Kamelia, they were willing to wait until she wasn't around. Allowing them a little time to bond, Sno took a piece of meat off the grill, and turned to look at Kash.

"So, Mr. Kashmir, what do you do for a living?"

"I have a few businesses I dabble in."

Sno raised one brow while nodding, quickly assuming he was into illegal things.

"That's a new name for it. I'ma have to use that." Chuckling, Sno was now very curious to know a little more about Kash. Sno knew the street life too well, and he knew where hood niggas who weren't living a legit life ended up. Fortunately for Sno, he had a good run in the game and was able to retire from his illegal job a wealthy man. Though he was on the police's radar in the past, he had never been to jail, and he was still alive to tell his story. However, Sno knew that was rare. He knew that fate wasn't something every nigga in the game got a chance to live through and speak on.

Opening the top to the barbecue grill, Sno used the tongs to remove a few burgers. Placing it into a pan, he tapped Kash's chest and motioned his head towards the house.

"Come on… Kamelia, go over there with your mama."

"Okay, Papa." Kamelia climbed down, and Kash followed Sno to the house.

When they entered, Sno sat the food down on the counter in the kitchen. Kash was silent. Sno went into the fridge and took out a bottle of water.

"What do you drink with your liquor?" Sno asked, breaking the silence with the refrigerator still open, awaiting Kash's response.

"Water."

Sno pulled out an extra bottle of water, handed it to Kash, and Kash followed him into a room that looked like a full bar. Liquor bottles sat on a shelf behind a tall island with bright lights hanging above them. Stools were in front of it, as if Sno and Reign hosted parties in this very room all the time. A huge television hung from the wall, right above a fireplace. The spacious room was like something Kash had never seen before. The floor was carpeted, and the walls were grey and covered in pictures, both paintings and pictures of the family.

"You cool with Remy?" Sno asked, walking to the other side of the bar.

"Nah, man. That brown liquor is the devil." Laughing, Kash took a seat on the stool. "I'll fuck with that Azul."

"Aight, cool." Grabbing the bottle of Clase Azul Tequila and two glasses, Sno decided he would drink that too. He didn't usually drink anything other than Remy, but he was attempting to make Kash feel comfortable. This conversation was long overdue. Removing the lid, Sno poured them both a glass. He picked up the remote to the TV, turned it on, and rap music began to play.

Now that they were alone, Kash was ready to talk. It was clear that Sno didn't know who he was other than being Heaven's baby daddy. But after Kash found out the homie Dre always talked about was Heaven's father, he needed to let him know he'd been a long-time employee of the family business. He was a part of the Chicago branch. He worked very closely with Dre, and he was the nigga who killed the agents.

"Your crib is nice. I plan to buy Heaven and Kamelia something like this real soon."

"Is that right?"

"Yeah, man." Kash took a sip from his glass.

"How do you plan on affording it? I know you said you dabble in different things, but what are those things?"

"Honestly, I work with Dre. He's like a big brother to me. For years now, I've been running a few spots in Chicago for him. I didn't even know you and Heaven's father were the same person until Dre asked me to look over his partner's daughter. So, when I say I dabble in different things, my resume is long as fuck. I've done a lot of shit for money. From heinous shit, to running a few stash spots, to petty shit. You name it, I've probably done it."

"Hassan and Bullock?"

"Yeah, man, that shit was fascinating as fuck," he said, chuckling, thinking back to how loud the explosion was. The bomb fucked the agents up so bad, and he knew they didn't see the hit coming. It was the riskiest shit ever, but exciting nonetheless. Dre paid him a million to kill the agents, and he stored the money away, after paying Lance $200,000 just for coming with him.

"Did Dre know you were Kamelia's father?"

"Nah, he still doesn't know. I haven't said anything about me and Heaven to him. That has been the furthest thing from my mind. Lately, I've been focused on me and Heaven, tryna see where me and her relationship can go."

Sno nodded his head as he silently listened to Kash talk.

"Look, I know I fucked up in the past with Heaven. I regret that shit every day. I know you brought me in here to have a heart to heart on being a father, but I don't need that. I just want to leave the past behind me and get to know my daughter without any pushback."

"Nah, you won't get any pushback from me as long as you treat my daughter and granddaughter right, understanding that when shit gets tough, you're not going to fold and leave them to fend for themselves all over again. I have all the money in the world. I can give them whatever they want and need, but I'm only a father. I can't mend her broken heart. I can't fill the void of someone she feels should be there to help her. You feel me?"

"Yeah, I understand. And yeah, that was fucked up how I just walked out of her life, but I was twenty-one, and Heaven was only sixteen. She lied to me about her age. I had to walk away when I found out the truth. I couldn't be with shorty. That shit made me feel like a fucking pedophile. Her dishonesty could've cost me my life. If I had to make that decision all over again, I would leave again, but I wouldn't stay away for as long as I did. I would come looking for my daughter sooner."

Sno was able to hear Kash out in that instance, but if this was five years ago, Kamelia would probably be fatherless because Sno would've killed him. Twenty-one and sixteen was a huge age gap. Kash was too old to be sexing Heaven, and Heaven was too young to even be thinking about sex.

"I hear the sincerity in your voice, mane. Don't beat yourself up over the past. We've all made mistakes. Just make sure you keep my granddaughter your number one priority from this day forward. She deserves that. Show her what a real man looks like, so when she becomes an adult, she won't make dumb ass mistakes."

"I'm on the job."

The two men shook hands and drank their drinks down. Afterwards, they went back outside and sat around the pool with Heaven and Reign. Taking a seat on the lawn chairs, they watched the kids as they talked. Heaven sat in the chair between Kash and Sno while Reign sat on Sno's lap. He caressed Reign's back, and Heaven smiled at the two. For as long as she could remember, they had always been this way. They were two people in love, who expressed their adoration in front of whoever whenever. Everyone sat there quietly, obviously in their own heads, thinking their own personal thoughts.

"So, what's been going on over here?"

"Nothing really. It's been pretty quiet. Your grandma, KeKe, has been over, her and King. That's about it."

"No Delilah?"

"Nah, by now I'm sure you know that I know about your mama and that nigga she was fucking around with when she got pregnant with Delilah."

"Yes, I know. Still, Daddy, you're the only father she knows. You can't just turn your back on her."

"I haven't turned my back on her. I just need time to process everything. I love that little girl so much, mane, and I know that shit is going to devastate me if she's not my daughter."

"It's going to devastate all of us," Reign said.

"I'm trying to work my way into actually establishing paternity. Either way, she's my daughter, and I want full custody. That Bully character is on his death bed. Delilah still needs me, either as a father or just a male role model, but I'm done funding Anika. She gotta figure that shit out for herself. Shit, the house I bought her is paid off, and the deed is in her name. She better sell that motherfucka because Bank Sno is officially closed."

"If you need me to, I will take a paternity test too. I mean, I know you are my father, but I don't want you to have questions or doubts. My mama is such a fucked-up person."

"Nah, Sweet Pea. I have no questions or doubts. You are my daughter."

"Well, I need to go check on my house."

Heaven stood as well as Kash. They were going to stop by Heaven's house so that she could break things off with Derrick, and afterwards, they would stay the night in a hotel suite.

They walked into a quiet house, with Derrick sitting on the couch, fully dressed and his bags packed, sitting by the front door. It was as if he knew Heaven and Kash were on their way.

When the two men met, they greeted one another with a quick handshake as Heaven and Kash took a seat on the loveseat.

The conversation with Derrick went well. As

requested, Heaven allowed Kash to be there while she broke things off with him. He told her that he figured she had moved on when she stopped answering his calls, and he was cool with it as long as she and Kamelia were happy.

"Aye, I understand. I been knew things were over between us, but I do want to let you know that, while you were gone, your mother tried to come over here. She had been flirting with me, making me feel uncomfortable and shit." He conveniently left the part out where Anika sucked his dick.

"My mama is a nasty, trifling bitch, and I don't want anything to do with her. If you want, you can be with her."

"Hell naw, mane. I just thought you should know."

She let him know that he was welcome to stay in the house for as long as he needed to because she would be going back to Chicago until the end of the year.

FIFTEEN

Heaven laughed as Kash and Kamelia had a pillow fight on the couch while she stood in the entryway with her arms across her chest. Their father and daughter relationship was so cute. They had been stuck at the hip since the day they met each other.

Heaven could honestly say that she was happy with the decision she had made to pursue love with a man she swore she would hate forever. She knew from the day they reunited that they would end up in a relationship. They just had to work out the kinks of their past. Plus, Kamelia fell in love with him the first time she saw him. It was like she was mesmerized. From the way Kamelia just stared at him while he held her to the way she wiped Kash's tears after he broke out crying.

Kash hit Kamelia with the decorative pillow he held in his hand, which sent Kamelia flying backwards on her butt. She laughed and stood back up, ready to attack, but Kash hit her again.

"Daddy, let me hit you back!" Yelling, Kamelia had, had enough. She swung her pillow hard at Kash and hit him in his eye.

He fell on the floor, pretending to be hurt, and Kamelia jumped on his back. "Aahhh, shit!"

"Kash, you can't be cussing in front of her. You already know how her mouth is set up."

"Damn, my bad, baby. Kamelia, I don't want to hear you saying shit. Okay?" he said, but Kamelia didn't respond. She just stood from Kash's back and climbed on the couch, ready to him him with the pillow again. "Kamelia?"

"Huh?"

"Did you hear me?"

"Mmhmm."

"Then why didn't you respond?" Heaven asked.

"Because Daddy said he didn't want to hear me say shit," she said honestly, putting her hand to her mouth and laughing.

"You see! Don't say it again."

"Why not?" Kamelia bounced down on the couch with her arms crossed. "Daddy said it first."

"G, leave my baby alone. I did say I didn't want to

hear her say shit." He got up, grabbed Kamelia, picked her up over his head, and slammed her onto the couch. He tickled her.

"I'ma be calling your ass all the way to Atlanta when she gets in trouble for cussing in school."

"And I'ma be on the first flight to check whoever, my nigga." He walked over to Heaven. Putting his elbow and forearm to the wall, he leaned down and kissed Heaven's forehead. Kamelia ran up behind him and grabbed his leg. He reached down for her and picked her up. Now, he had both of his girls with him. He pecked Kamelia's cheek, and she laid her head on his shoulder. They both looked at Heaven with the same exact expression on their faces.

"Ugh, y'all ass look just alike."

"What you mean ugh? Baby K, what she mean ugh, like we ugly?" Kamelia hunched her shoulders. "G, I'ma handsome nigga, and my baby girl is gorgeous. She get her looks from me."

"Conceited much?" Heaven reached up and cupped Kash's chin. "You are fine though." She pulled his face to her and kissed his lips.

The sound of Kash's alarm going off stopped their cute little moment. He quickly put Kamelia down and went into the bedroom to retrieve his gun and car keys.

"Go in the room and close the door," he told

Heaven as he made his way to the front door.

Heaven was so nosey because she could have sworn Esha and even Kash told her that he didn't bring people to his home. Somehow, someone was outside messing with one of his cars.

Heaven picked Kamelia up and took her into the bedroom. She sat her down on the bed and ran back to the bedroom door to peek out. She watched as Kash opened the door and stepped out. He hit the alarm to his Tesla while looking from left to right.

"Is everything okay, Kash?" Heaven yelled out as she stepped from the room and began to walk towards the door with Baby Kamelia right behind her.

"Yeah, everything is cool," he said, looking at his Camaro that was parked across the street from his home. He stood out there for a few more seconds before going back inside. "It probably was a cat or something."

"Yeah, it probably was a tiger," Kamelia said, grabbing Kash's leg and roaring.

"Silly." Heaven laughed.

The doorbell rang, and Kash turned around. He walked back to the door and said, "Who is it?"

"Asia," she boldly said.

Kash looked back at Heaven, confusingly. He knew

for a fact he had never brought Asia to his home. So, how did she know where he lived? Opening the door, with Kamelia right on the side of him, he frowned.

She looked crazy and deranged. Her face was red and swollen from crying, still a weird smile was on her face. She tried wrapping her arms around Kash to hug him, but he pushed her back.

Heaven stood in place, allowing Kash to handle his crazy ex. She knew he had it covered, so she didn't intervene just yet.

"Asia, what the fuck are you doing here?"

"I came to check on you. I haven't seen you in a while. I thought you would be happy to see me."

"You didn't think no shit like that. I got my family here, Asia. You need to leave."

"Your family?" She scoffed. Looking down to the left of him, she saw Kamelia standing there, looking up at her. "Your fucking family, Kashmir? So, they are your family now? What about me and my kids? What the fuck are we?"

Putting his hand to Kamelia's chest, he pushed her back and behind himself, shielding her from the meltdown Asia was sure to have.

Heaven began to walk towards them. The way Asia was letting the 'fuck' word fly from her mouth, as if her daughter wasn't standing there, had Heaven pissed. She knew Kash had it handled, but her motherly instinct pushed her to the front door.

"Man, Asia, don't you see my daughter standing here? Watch your mouth, man."

"Kash, how could you do this to me? I had to stalk you to find out where you live, but you let this bitch and her child move in with no problem."

"Asia…"

Without a word, Heaven walked around Kash and slapped Asia in her mouth. Before things could escalate further, he pulled her back inside the house. He got in between the two ladies, but Heaven didn't want to fight. She just wanted to shut Asia's cry baby ass up.

Asia stood there with her hand to her mouth in shock. She looked up at Kash with tears in her eyes. She couldn't believe Heaven had just hit her.

"You let her hit me, Kash."

"He told you to watch your mouth in front of my daughter!" Heaven yelled. She picked Kamelia up and put her on her hip and walked over to the couch. "Get her away from this house, Kash."

Kash pulled the door closed as Asia yelled out. "Bitch, fuck you and your daughter!"

"Asia, G, you a fucking joke. You come over here, disrespecting my household, my daughter, my girl. Get the fuck on. You did this shit to yourself."

"Your daughter? Your girl?" She was aghast, hearing those words come from his mouth. He said it with so much pride, as if they were the highlight of his life.

"Yes, my daughter and girl. What part of us being over don't you understand? You need to be at home, focusing on your own kids, building a bond and relationship with them."

"Fuck you, Kash. I got something for your ass." She descended the stairs and walked to her Subaru.

Kash watched as she opened the door, causing the lights to come on inside the SUV. Seeing Malaysia, India, and Taiwan inside, Kash shook his head. It was sad how she brought her kids to his house with her knowing things would more than likely go left.

She started up her ignition and crazily pulled from her parking spot. Her tires screeched loudly as she maneuvered around the car parked in front of her. In less than thirty seconds, she was doing sixty miles per hour down the block. By the time she reached a stop sign, she was at a hundred, and it was too late for her to slow down or stop. Blowing straight through it, she ran into a small Mack truck, instantly killing herself and her kids on impact. A loud explosion erupted through the air, and the foul stench of metal and rubber filled Kash's nostrils.

He ran out into the street, just as Heaven opened the front door and followed behind him with Kamelia on her hip. They both ran down the block with Heaven stopping a few paces behind him.

Seeing a mangled Malaysia on the ground next to the truck, Heaven covered Kamelia's eyes. This was just too much.

Kash became emotional. His eyes filled with tears, seeing her like this. He had really grown an attachment to Asia's kids over the past months. Malaysia was a sweet kid. She caught the most slack but still made sure her siblings were okay. She'd suffered through a lot, but now, it was all over. All three of Asia's children were well behaved and sweet. To see this scene was breaking Kash's heart.

Kneeling next to Malaysia, he yelled for Heaven to call the police as the block began to fill with onlookers.

Malaysia's eyes were wide open but lifeless. He used his hand to close them before sitting on the ground next to her. For a long while, he sat there, helplessly, with tears running down his face. He couldn't help but to think this was all his fault. It wasn't until Heaven walked over and touched his shoulder did he get up. A few seconds earlier, she asked one of the neighbors to keep an eye on Kamelia while she checked on Kash. He looked down at her and wrapped his arms around her tightly. His grief-stricken face made her misty eyed. She knew he would need time to get through this, so she planned to be there for him every step of the way.

EPILOGUE

One Year Later

Sno and Anika's Appearance

On Paternity Court

"Good luck, bae," Reign said, hugging and kissing Sno. She ran her hand down his black sweater and gray stripped, black slacks, dusting him off before she took her place on the side of him. Today, she was here to be a witness; however, she looked more like his lawyer, dressed in a Cinq à Sept Victorian inspired, high neck, long sleeved, black dress with ruffles on the shoulder, sleeves, and around the base of the bottom. Black tights hid her thick thighs, and a pair of black Sergio Rossi, embellished mesh pumps added a little more elegance to her look. Her hair was pulled back into a tight ponytail, that was parted down the middle, and her makeup was natural. Reign was seven months pregnant. Her belly was a nice size, and she carried it well.

"Thank you, baby." Biting down on his bottom lip and wiping underneath it, he turned around and intertwined his fingers before placing them on top of the stand. He said a silent praying, begging God that he was, in fact, the father of Delilah. He loved her to death, just like the rest of his kids, but in the back of his mind, he knew she wasn't.

Nervous jitters plagued him as he stood there, staring straight forward. He had been trapped in his own thoughts for a while now, thinking what if. What if he grew an attachment to a child who wasn't his? What if he wasted time spent with a child who wasn't his? It was never about the money for him. He had plenty of that, but what if he put his all into loving a child who wasn't his? Sno sighed and looked over at Reign, who also seemed to be deep in thought. He rubbed her back before squaring his shoulders and cupping one fist with the other in front of him. He was ready, but he wasn't sure if he was ready to talk about ten years ago. That shit there was old news.

"Mmm!" Anika was staring enviously at Sno and Reign. She pursed her lips together and popped her tongue. "I should've known you was going to bring your little wife with you. Pussy ass. Congratulations on the little bastard." She smirked. "Nigga can't do shit without his mammy or his bald head ass wife."

Sno chuckled, but he didn't respond. Anika was

one bitter woman. He removed his fist hand from his other hand and touched the small of Reign's back. She looked up at him, in his eyes. Sno shook his head no, signaling for her to stay calm and not react to Anika's comment. She was clearly trying to create a distraction.

Reign listened, only responding with a deep sigh. She looked past Sno and over at Anika, scowling. Her little comments didn't really get to Reign. For some reason, she knew Delilah wasn't Sno's daughter, and she knew Anika knew this as well, specifically because her nervousness was showing. She smirked because, in the end, she would get the last laugh. Reign watched as Anika stood at the podium, tapping her long, black claws against the wood. The bitch was so ghetto and ratchet. She looked like a hood rich chick with big ass gold hoops in her ears, as if she was going to an eighties party, instead of court. Who would really take this girl serious? She looked like a fake ass Nicki Minaj with her long, Ombre, bleach blonde and pink wig all the way down to the blue jean dress and sparkly Louboutin pumps she wore.

"Ratchet ass," Reign whispered. Smirking, she turned and looked forward. Soon enough, those Wright checks would no longer be funding Anika's lifestyle, and Reign couldn't wait.

"You good?" Sno asked, looking at Reign.

"Yeah, I'm fine. These boys are kicking my ass though."

Sno smiled and put his hand to Reign's stomach, feeling his baby boys move around. He couldn't wait to meet them. They were identical twins, and he knew these two were going to look exactly like him.

Finally, the cameras were cued, and the judge came out from the back.

"Please be seated," the judge said as she took a seat behind the bench. Judge Lauren Lake was a beautiful woman with chocolate brown skin, long hair, and beautiful dimples in her cheeks. Today, she looked excited to be taking on this case. Looking to her bailiff, she smiled. Her lips were covered in a purplish lipstick. The way she smiled, it was like she already knew the results.

"Good morning, Your Honor. This is the case of Wright versus Davidson."

"Thank you, Jerome," the judge said. "Everyone, please be seated..." Shuffling papers, she looked at Sno. "Good morning, Mr. and Mrs. Wright, Miss Davidson."

"Good morning, Your Honor," Sno, Reign, and Anika said in unison.

"So, Mr. Wright, you say that Ms. Davidson has led you to believe that her ten-year-old daughter, Delilah, is your child, and you've been taking care of her since she was born, but recently, another man has come forward, claiming that he is, in fact, Delilah's father.

But if Delilah is your daughter, you want full custody. Is that correct, Mr. Wright?"

"Yes, Your Honor."

"Ms. Davidson, you claim that the other man is lying, you were not dealing with anyone else when you conceived, and Mr. Wright is, in fact, the father of Delilah. Right, Ms. Davidson?"

"Yes, ma'am!" Anika replied, cocking her head to the side, pursing her lips together, and looking over at Sno.

"Okay, Mr. Wright, tell the court what happened to make you question paternity."

"Honestly, Your Honor, Delilah's paternity has always been in question since the day Ms. Davidson told me she was pregnant. At the time, we weren't together. About six years prior, we were engaged, but things happened where we ended up just going our separate ways. A lot of things make me question if Delilah is my daughter. For instance, when my wife was pregnant with our five-year-old twins, Ms. Davidson was telling Delilah that my unborn babies weren't her siblings, and most importantly, another man is claiming to be Delilah's father." Sno explained with his hands still in front of him. He was cool and calm as he talked.

"Stop lying, Demarco! That didn't even happen. Ain't no man came to you and told you nothing,"

Anika yelled, frowning. "My baby became a question when you got with that bi…"

"Ms. Davidson! Now, what we are not going to do is disrespect anyone. I understand you are upset, but you will not use foul language in my court room. Understood?"

"Yes." She rolled her eyes.

"Now, Miss Davidson, who is Donterio Brown?"

"This guy I used to kick it with back in the day."

"Isn't it true he might be the father?"

"No, Demarco Wright is Delilah Wright's father, and he knows it. If he had questions about my baby's paternity, why is he just now asking for a test?"

"Well, Mr. Wright, Miss Davidson has a point. If Delilah's paternity has always been in question, what made you wait ten long years to get answers?" With a frown on her face, the judge sat up curiously. "Is Mrs. Wright the reason you and Ms. Davidson went your separate ways? And is she the reason you are now questioning paternity?"

"No, ma'am, Judge. I was not dealing with my wife at the time Ms. Davidson and I were together. I'm not that type of man. I just didn't have the heart to know the truth. Over the years, I've grown an attachment to her. I treat Delilah like the rest of my kids."

"How many kids do you have, Mr. Wright?"

"I have four, including Delilah, and two on the way."

"Naw, don't include Delilah. Like you said, you don't know if she is yours." Anika pursed her lips together and tapped her nails on the table.

"This girl is nuts," Reign mumbled.

"Bitch, what? I don't give a damn about you being pregnant or about us being in the courtroom," Anika yelled.

"You're jealous of me. That's what it really is," Reign said, laughing. "Don't be mad at me because your daughter told me your secret."

"Don't argue with her, Reign," Frowning, Sno turned to Reign. He was pissed. He moved his hand as he talked. "You know I'm not with all this, mane." He was embarrassed. They were on national TV, acting a whole fool.

"Like I said, I love Delilah to death. In my mind, she is my daughter, but when I have to hear about Ms. Davidson sneaking up to prisons with my daughter and telling her that another man is her father, that becomes a problem for me. I've been in Delilah's life since before she was born. When it came to my kids, I took Anika's word for it," Sno said.

"Yeah, right, Demarco. You know Delilah is your daughter."

"Does he, Ms. Davidson?"

"Yes, he does, Judge. He knows Delilah is his. I've been knowing Demarco since I was sixteen years old." She moved her hands and fingers as she talked. "We have a twenty-one-year-old daughter together. He is not the type of man to take care of another man's baby." She looked at Sno and hit her hand up against the podium. "Now, tell me I'm lying!"

Sno smirked, silently shaking his head and hanging it low. Anika was dumb as fuck. He had to figure out how the hell he let Reign talk him into coming here. Anika was an embarrassment.

"Mr. Wright?" Judge Lake looked at him questioning.

"How would she know what I would do? I haven't been with a woman who has kids outside the children we created together." He frowned and scoffed loudly.

Reign sighed. She blamed Sno for everything they were going through. For everything Anika had put them and their marriage through. Honestly, with all the doubt he had in his heart, this paternity test should've happened a long time ago. The entire time Anika and Sno talked, Reign was silent; however, there was so much she wanted to say, but she didn't want to get riled up.

"Clearly, he would take care of another man's baby if he has taken care of Delilah for ten years." Reign chimed in.

"What are you saying, Mrs. Wright?"

"Girl, you just saying anything," Anika said.

"All of Demarco's kids has some type of feature of his, whether it's his hair, smile, or whole face. Delilah, although I love her to death, and I will always love her, does not look like my husband at all."

"Do you agree with that, Mr. Wright?"

"Yes, I absolutely agree. Honestly, at the time Anika got pregnant, we weren't together anymore, but she made it easy for me to come through and hit her…"

"And still is," Anika said, raising one brow.

"Anika, mane, stop lying. I haven't been with you in years," he said, finally addressing her.

"Years? Well, what happened at your mama house a few months ago?" The entire room gasped.

"Girl, you wish my husband will give you the time of day. Your Honor, this girl is such a liar. She lies about everything. She has been doing all she can to ruin me and Mr. Wright's marriage!" Reign yelled.

"Nothing happened between me and you a few months ago."

"So, nothing happened when your wife was in Chicago?"

Sno sucked his teeth. "Hell naw." He waved her off.

"Wait, wait!" The judge frowned. "Mr. Wright, is this true?"

"My wife knows about Anika sneaking into my parents' house while I was sleep and trying to have sex with me. But that has nothing to do with this paternity test."

"I've never met a woman so desperate that she has to rape a man. She is a poor excuse of a woman."

Whispers and gasps rumbled throughout the room as Sno explained what happened.

"I didn't have to rape him. This man has been begging to have sex with me for years." She lied.

"Bitch!" Reign said. She was so tired of Anika.

"Calm down, baby." Sno grabbed a hold of Reign's face at her chin, forcing her to look at him. "You're pregnant, mane. I told you not to argue with her. You know me, and you know damn well she is lying."

"Right, tell your bitch to shut the fuck up, Demarco, because you already know you can't control shit over here."

The judge banged her gavel, but that didn't stop

anything. Reign, feeling slighted, continued to exchange words with Anika. Anika was right. Sno always expected her to be the bigger person while Anika did and said whatever she wanted to. In that moment, she wasn't worried about her babies and the stress she was putting on herself. She was going to get her point across.

"You are so jealous of me, Anika. The shit is just sick and sad. I got the man and the kids while you telling a nigga that is in jail that he's the father of your daughter. You're a dumb bitch. If you was smart, you would've kept collecting them checks and shut the fuck up." Sno looked at Reign in bewilderment. Although she was telling the truth, he just never expected any of this to come from her. "I got the life you want. You mad ass bitch. You got the right one. Messing with me, you gon' forever be mad."

Before the judge could gain order in the courtroom, an argument between Reign and Anika broke out. Anika pointed her long painted nails, and Reign pointed hers as well, while Sno and Jerome stood in between the two, trying to gain control of the entire situation. Anika was escorted out, while Reign took a seat behind Sno. They took a thirty-minute break to calm everyone down before bringing Anika back into the room.

"Whew, welcome back." The judge blew out a breath. "You know, I've been in this business for a long time, and when dealing with family and paternity, things can get a little emotional, like we just witnessed here. I tell you, Mr. Wright, I would surely hate to be you, especially if things like this happen all the time…"

"Your Honor," Anika said, raising her hand, "I just want to apologize. I allowed my feelings to get the best of me." Anika spoke in a baby voice.

"Thank you, Ms. Davidson, but I'm reluctant to believe this isn't how you act on a regular."

"This is the type of stuff she does, Your Honor. She antagonizes a situation and then apologizes. This is what I have to deal with on the regular with her, and I'm sick of it. I just want to know if Delilah is mine or not."

"Before we get to the test, we have a guest via satellite." Everyone turned to the TV screen, and Bully's sickly face appeared.

"What is he doing here?" Anika sucked her teeth.

"Thank you for joining us, Mr. Brown. Can you give us a little background on you and Ms. Davidson's relationship?"

"Well, I met her at a club years ago while she was engaged to Mr. Wright, but we didn't start talking until they were broken up. Eventually, we started dating and having a sexual relationship. I was pretty much living with her, taking care of her and her oldest daughter."

"You had this man living in the house I bought for you and my daughter?" Frowning, Sno chuckled.

"Look, mane, I didn't mean any disrespect. From my understanding, y'all were done. I had no idea y'all were still having sex. I went to jail, and she told me she was pregnant. I guess that's why it was so easy for her to lead both me and Mr. Wright on."

Anika sucked her teeth again, rolling her eyes.

"What's wrong, Ms. Davidson? Is Mr. Brown lying? Was Mr. Wright the only man you were with at the time of conception?"

"No, he's not lying. Donterio and I were intimate, but Demarco was the only man I was with when I conceived," she lied.

"Remember, you are under oath. Are you sure?"

"Yes."

"Okay. Let's get the results. This test was performed by DNA Diagnostics, and they read as follows. When it comes to ten-year-old, Delilah Wright, Ms. Davidson, Mr. Wright is not this child's father. Mr. Brown is."

The room filled with dismay as Sno laid his head on his arms on the podium and cried. Reign stood up from her seat. She walked up to the side of him and rubbed his back.

"Ms. Davidson," the judge shook her head, "what do you have to say? You knew Mr. Wright wasn't the father."

"No, I didn't know he wasn't the father. But oh well!"

"What do you mean oh well?"

"My daughter doesn't need a father as long as she has me."

That was all Heaven needed to see before she turned the TV off. She stood from the couch with tears pouring down her face. It had been months since the show was filmed; nonetheless, seeing her father hurt hurt her. She wanted to fight Anika in that very moment as she walked to the kitchen and over to the fridge before opening it and pulling out a package of ground chicken. Her emotions were too much right now, especially since she was pregnant and due any day now. With her baby boy, Kashmir Harris Jr., still holding up space in her belly, she couldn't indulge in a glass of Remy to help her calm down. Thus far, her pregnancy had been beautiful. Finally getting the opportunity to enjoy the creation of her baby with the man who helped create it, she had been happy. But seeing her mother make a fool of her father on television, she was fuming.

She needed to preoccupy her mind with something, and cooking dinner would have to do. Sitting the meat down, she stood there with her hands on her hips, in deep contemplation. She wanted to call Sno and talk to him, but she didn't want to reopen old wounds.

Yes, she already knew Delilah wasn't her father's daughter; still, watching the foolery play out on TV was embarrassing. She couldn't believe the damage Anika had caused them all. It was sad how she disregarded everyone's feelings to make herself feel good. Now, Heaven questioned her own paternity. She wanted to know if Sno was her father as well, but she didn't want to play with fire. She went twenty -two years with him being her father, and she preferred to leave it that way. The chaos Anika caused them was crazy. She knew this whole time there was a possibility Sno wasn't Delilah's father. Still, she put on a whole charade on national television.

With tears still falling from her eyes, she managed to prep her food while trying to compose herself. She didn't even know what she was about to cook, still she walked over to the sink. She washed her hands before grabbing a glass bowl from the cupboard. Afterwards, she picked out her seasonings. Opening the meat by poking a hole in the plastic film, she just stood there again, staring at everything she had laid out on the counter. She thought about how her mother hadn't taught her shit about being a woman. Everything she learned was from either her grandmother, KeKe, or stepmother, Reign. How could Anika be so selfish? She took a deep breath, closed her eyes, and sulked, counting to ten as she breathed in and out slowly. She heard her front door open as Kash and Kamelia entered her apartment. Hurriedly, she wiped her tears, turned around, and smiled.

"Hey, my loves," Heaven said, reaching down as Kamelia ran to her with chocolate ice cream all over her face. She hugged Heaven and wiped her mouth all over Heaven's shirt. "Ewww, Kamelia."

"Sorry." She laughed.

"You good, baby?" Kash asked as he approached her with one hand behind his back. He rubbed her belly and kissed her lips. "How is KJ doing?"

"We're good. I talked to Esha and Nadia earlier. Both of them swear I am going to go into labor tonight. We have a three hundred dollar bet between the three of us."

"Yeah?" Kash asked. "Nah, my boy ain't ready to come out yet. Maybe in a few days."

"That's the same thing I said."

"Mommy, look at what we have." Kamelia walked behind Kash and took the sandy brown baby Pomeranian from his hand. "It's a doggy."

"Kash, I fucking hate dogs," she whispered.

"It's not for you to like. He's Baby K's anyways."

Heaven rolled her eyes. "Awww, it is so cute."

"Yes, he is. His name is Dusty."

"Mmm."

"Here, hold him, Mommy," Kamelia demanded, and Kash laughed. He hugged Heaven before walking away.

"Naw, no thanks, baby. I'm about to cook. I'll hold Dusty later. But put him down and go wash your face."

It was now September 2021. Now that they were in a committed relationship, they made it a tradition to stay majority of the year in Atlanta and spend June through October in Chicago. So, she asked Sno to renew her lease. Now, they took turns staying at his house and her apartment. Heaven was excited to see what the rest of their lives together would bring. They had been through a lot, but in the end, Heaven received what she came to Chicago for - Kash's heart and time.

A few days later, as Kash and Heaven predicted, Heaven was pushing Kashmir Jr. out. He was born September 14th at 6:20 a.m., weighing eight pounds even.

They were now complete. They were still working towards the last name part, but they weren't rushing anything. In the meantime, they planned to discover new ways to love each other and raise their children in a two-parent household.

***

After the show, Anika gave up her maternal rights to Delilah and checked herself into a mental institute.

Needless to say, after she lost Sno for good, she really lost her mind. She knew she needed help. Soon after their appearance on Paternity Court, Bully passed away from his illness.

Initially, Heaven was going to get full custody of Delilah, but after Reign birthed two beautiful baby boys at only thirty-three weeks of pregnancy, Sno and Reign stepped up and took on the responsibility. Sno still loved Delilah, as if she was his own, and he didn't want to separate her from the rest of the kids. With a houseful of babies and children, their family was now complete.

THE
END